M000206006

The Fighter

Paul "Doc" Gaccione

Brighton Publishing LLC
435 N. Harris Drive
Mesa, AZ 85203

The Fighter

Paul "Doc" Gaccione

Brighton Publishing LLC
435 N. Harris Drive
Mesa, AZ 85203

www.brightonpublishing.com

ISBN13: 978-1-62183-568-4

Printed in the United States of America

First Edition

Cover Design: Tom Rodriguez

Other Books by Paul "Doc" Gaccione

AVAILABLE WHEREVER FINE BOOKS ARE SOLD

"BEYOND THE BEYOND:"

MY JOURNEY TO DESTINY

2011 — ISBN: 978-1-936587-52-0

"THE GODFATHER OF SOULS"

2016 — ISBN: 978-1-62183-406-9

"THE GREAT ESCAPE:"

THE INSIDE STORY OF THE

DANNEMORA PRISON ESCAPE

2017 — 978-1-62183-448-9

"THE PSYCHO CLUB"

2019 — ISBN: 978-1-62183-516-5

Dedication

I DEDICATE THIS BOOK TO MY PRECIOUS ELEVEN
GRANDCHILDREN

Acknowledgements

KIM OREFICE KIST, WHOSE TIRELESS HELP ENABLED ME
TO WRITE MY LAST FIVE BOOKS.

Special Gratitude

TOM CIARDELLA AND JOHN LIUZZI

I WOULD LIKE TO SHOW SPECIAL GRATITUDE TO MY TWO
DEAR FRIENDS FOR THEIR SUPPORT IN THE WRITING OF MY
BOOKS.

Publisher's Note

THIS BOOK CONTAINS THE AUTHOR'S ORIGINAL UNEDITED
WORDS AS WRITTEN.

Author's Quotes

"To our most precious treasure that has given us life, we call this gift Mother."

"I cry out to be heard, for there is much to be said, and destiny has shown me the words to say."

"To be able to see light even in darkness is truly a blessing and for this reason is why I write."

"I have to remind myself that I have not chosen writing, but writing has chosen me."

"Throughout my life I have tried my very best to be whatever I wanted to be, BUT FAILED, now in the twilight of my life, I see, that I have succeeded, just knowing that I have tried my very best."

"It really sucks getting old, but what a true blessing it is, to be alive, to have the experience."

"Words are impressive, but actions are convincing."

ᑬᐧᖫᕫIntroductionᕫᐧᑭ

T his is an incredible story about an old man who has just recently had his conviction overturned after spending seven years in prison.

Despite being kept from his loved ones for all that time, he has no animosity being that he is such a strong believer in his destiny.

Perhaps there is no animosity being that the old man hadn't wasted a single day of his incarceration. Along with penning four bestsellers he had spent countless hours through those years mentoring and giving hope and encouragement to countless inmates.

This story is about an old man that is so determined to bring forth a message that he is ready to risk his life.

During the story, there is this one incredible unexplainable event that takes place which will keep you on your toes throughout.

This story offers some humor and many messages, but most of all, it shows that an unbreakable determination in one's belief in destiny, one way or another will somehow be fulfilled.

Foreword

My insight is telling me that it's time to start writing my next book. I have been patiently waiting for some time to receive the inspiration that is needed for me to be able to write.

Just like all my other books that I have written I'm only able to write when the inspiration comes upon me, and then, and only then, are the words able to be written.

I say in my first book that it was only after a few special occurrences had occurred in my life that I was inspired to write my first book despite never having read a book.

I make the claim that only through the inspiration that is given to me am I able to be given the insight to write. I have noticed that throughout the writing of all my books, each time a story was told it was to bring forth a message that I was inspired to tell.

It was easy for me to see that I had not chosen writing, but that writing had chosen me.

I will start this story by mentioning that as I was at my desk writing my first book; there were twenty FBI and New York Organized Crime Task Force agents busting into my home to arrest me on a mafia hit that they say occurred twenty years earlier.

They claimed that I am a member of the mafia, which I vigorously deny. I was indicted and arrested in April of 2010 for murder. They say that I drove the van where the shooting took place. I spent six months at the infamous Rikers Island jail before being released on a one-million-dollar bail.

Two years later I was brought to trial. The prosecution had absolutely no evidence against me. How could they, if I was innocent?

The only evidence that the prosecution provided was two State witnesses, John Leto and John Mamone. John Leto testified that he was the shooter and that I was the driver.

John Mamone testified that I told him about the hit after picking him up at the airport. Mamone was a partner of mine in my physical fitness invention.

Could it be a coincidence that they were both facing life in prison for trafficking a load of marijuana and were set free for their testimony?

Could it also be a coincidence that they were both past convicted perjurers?

I had provided my lawyer with such overwhelming evidence to prove the two state's witnesses were lying and yet my lawyer chose not to put on a defense.

Although I knew he was wrong, I was preoccupied with the publishing of my first book. My writing had become my entire life. Truth be told, I couldn't take these charges seriously, how could they prove something that didn't happen?

When the jury walked into the courtroom after they had completed their deliberations, my lawyer leaned over to me and asked the question, "What do you think the verdict will be?" I looked into the jury box and said, "No doubt, the verdict is guilty."

Even though I knew that the sentence would be life, I looked directly into my lawyer's eyes and said, "The day will come when I will be speaking in front of 100,000 people in a stadium."

Now seven years have passed by, I have spent the first year of my incarceration at Auburn Prison, the oldest prison in the country and now the last six years here at Clinton Correctional Facility, one of the most notorious prisons in the country.

During this time of my incarceration, I have authored and published four bestselling books. Along with my writing, I have mentored countless inmates during this time.

Being such a strong believer in destiny, I have no doubt that destiny has brought me here to save some lives.

Recently my appeal lawyer has informed me that any day I could be getting a decision on whether I will be granted a hearing on my appeal. If so, I will be going to New York City to be in court for a hearing on my appeal.

In the meantime, I have decided to put all my work away and just anxiously wait to hear my fate as to being granted a hearing on my appeal.

During this time, I have met an interesting character. This inmate goes by the name of Little Nicky Ippolito. He was one of the major drug dealers out of Brooklyn in the eighties. He has been incarcerated for over twenty-nine years.

The interesting thing about meeting this man at this particular time is that he was capable of having some intellectual conversations with me. Even though he was seven years my junior, he was still able to relate to much of the same time in history as me.

The timing couldn't have been better for meeting this man than now while I have put all my work away and decided just to chill until I hear from the court.

Being such a strong believer in destiny, I have no doubt that this man came into my path for a purpose. After spending countless hours with this man and having deep philosophical conversations with him, I have seen that he has been blessed with a very special insight that has been given to only a few men.

ᢕᢧ᠊Chapter One᠊ᢗᢦᢓ

I usually wake up early and the next morning was no different. I was up and dressed, sitting on the edge of my bed and enjoying my first cup of joe when my cell gate opened. This happens at the same time every morning at 7:00 a.m.

Being the clerk of D-block Company, one of my responsibilities is to supervise the distribution of food trays to the inmates that are on disciplinary lockdown.

As I stepped out of my cell and began to walk down the tier, I was trying to figure out in my head what was on the menu for today. I then realized that we were having donuts for breakfast.

Yes! My favorite— today might not be such a bad day after all.

As I walked into the front corridor with a smile on my face, that's when I saw it. Out of my peripheral vision, driving straight toward the right side of my face a fist clocked me and that's when it hit me; I was being ambushed!

From my boxing experiences, even though it was too late to block the punch, I immediately counter with a left hook. Although it misses its target, my fist lands on the inmate's shoulder, he instantly fell to the ground.

1

No sooner than I threw that punch, I found two other inmates jumping on top of my back. To my surprise, I grabbed the one inmate that was on my back and threw him. He went flying through the air like he was a flash of light.

He flew through the air with such force that when he hit the wall, there was a thud that made you know that he was seriously injured.

As the third guy wound up to throw his right hand at my head, I blocked it with my left arm. I then did the same. I threw my right fist at his head and he blocked it with his left arm.

The amazing thing is that I hit him with such incredible force that I shattered all the bones in his arm. He instantly dropped to the ground with excruciating pain.

I couldn't believe that I destroyed all three of those young tough guys in less than sixty seconds. A seventy-two-year-old man just doesn't do this.

At that moment I blacked out, I assume I fainted from all the excitement. I did recollect hearing a few correctional officers (COs) saying, "I don't believe it, the old man broke the bones of all three of those inmates."

I then must have gone into an unconscious state because everything became a complete blank.

When I awoke, I found myself in an outside hospital lying in a bed with two correctional officers sitting in chairs, one on each side of me.

It seemed like it was only minutes after I regained consciousness when a sergeant came walking into the room and said to me, "If the doctor releases you, we are going to be transporting you to Downstate Prison. You are scheduled to be in court the day after tomorrow.

I immediately became overjoyed saying to myself, "I must have won the legal motion and I'm going to court because I have been granted a hearing."

When the doctor came into the room to examine me, I was going to do and say anything, whatever it would take for him to release me. After the doctor completed examining me, he said nothing as he left the room.

It seemed like an hour had passed when the sergeant walked back into the room and said to the COs, "Start getting him ready for the trip to Downstate Prison."

Downstate Correctional Facility is known to everyone in the New York prison system as a reception prison that acclimates all the new inmates to all the procedures of being in a maximum security prison.

After orientation has been completed, each inmate is finally shipped off to their assigned maximum prison.

Downstate also serves as the go-between facility for any inmates who need to appear in court in any of the five boroughs of New York City.

The two correctional officers (CO's) then started to put the leg shackles on my ankles. They then strapped a chain around my waist that was attached to the handcuffs that were put on my wrist.

After those two CO's escorted me down to the lobby of the hospital, there were two different CO's that were waiting to escort me to Downstate.

Unlike the first two CO's that work steady at the hospital guarding inmates that are coming in from all the different New York State Prisons, these two CO's were from Clinton Prison and they knew me.

After those two officers helped me into the van, we were headed to Downstate Prison. Two and a half hours later, approximately half-way to our destination, the CO's broke the silence, questioning me about the fight that I had with those three inmates that jumped me and landed me in the hospital.

The one CO asked me the question, "How in the hell does an old man like yourself beat the shit out of all three of those hoodlums?"

"Yea," the second CO piped in, "All three of them suffered broken bones and had to be taken to an outside hospital."

I could tell that these guys were in awe at the strength that I exhibited, especially knowing that I was age seventy-two. Even I could not explain to myself where all this exceptional strength came from.

Even though I had the same sentiment as the officers, I knew of my past physical abilities from years gone by. But nevertheless, I also felt it was hard to believe what I had done to those guys.

So, I answered the CO's by saying, "Part of me remembers my physical abilities and accomplishments of the past, but then again that was many, many years ago. I wasn't trying to hurt them CO, I was only trying to protect myself."

The other CO came back at me by saying that the prison investigator was dumb-founded when he noticed that two of the prison bars were bent on the gate for D-block. He then added that, ironically, that is exactly where you were jumped.

The other CO then said that the investigator put in his report that there is no mortal man on earth that is capable of having the strength to have bent those bars.

4

The investigator feels that this mystery is a serious problem for the security of the prison until they could come up with the answer.

I then replied to both the CO's by saying, "Surely you are not implying that I was the one who bent the bars?" We all got a good laugh at that comment.

When we arrived at Downstate to my surprise, there were many CO's that remembered me. I say that because it was six and a half years since I was last there. This was a comforting feeling and I suppose it's because back then many of the CO's had read my first book.

Despite the warm reception from the CO's that remembered me, the cold and hard reality of prison set in as I found myself locked in one of the many holding cells, also known as "bullpens." The facility was cold, and the cell reeked of stale urine. *"But it's only temporary,"* I told myself.

My nerves set in as it dawned on me that tomorrow morning, I'd be sitting in front of a judge arguing my case to be released from these chains.

That's when I asked myself the ultimate question, *Is that my destiny? Is it my destiny to finally beat these charges so that I can shed these chains and fulfill my life's mission? Or, I thought with a shudder, does my destiny lead me to fall victim to these bogus charges and instead of my two feet, will I be leaving these prison walls in a body bag?*

I truly believe that I've been successful in fulfilling a large portion of my journey to destiny. Over the course of my six and a half years incarcerated, I have dedicated my time and effort toward positivity.

When I'm not writing I focus my energy toward providing help and encouragement to inmates, spending countless hours mentoring others to find purpose and meaning in their lives.

In fact, every single inmate on my cellblock has displayed on their cell wall a motivational sign listing "DOC'S" FIVE INGREDIENTS TO SUCCESS IN LIFE. I'm proud of what I've been able to accomplish behind these walls, but I believe that my higher power has so much more in store for me.

In a way, this time that I've spent behind bars has been somewhat of a preparation course providing me with the necessary experiences and knowledge so that I am willing and able to fulfill my ultimate purpose in life.

Insight tells me that my final mission in life is to take all of the work that I've done while incarcerated and apply it on a much larger, grander scale. In essence, I am to spread my message to the masses beginning with the college and prison circuit.

My premonition is that my ultimate destiny will be fulfilled at Giant Stadium in front of 100,000 people as I reveal and discuss the message from Beyond the Beyond, a nonprofit corporation.

When the next morning arrived, I was up and about by 4:00 a.m. eating breakfast from a Styrofoam tray. Shortly after breakfast, officers were putting chains all around me to make the trip to New York City to be in court for 9:00 a.m.

When I was escorted into the courtroom, my appeal attorney, Mark Zeno was at the defense table waiting for me.

It was easy to notice when I saw a female sitting at the prosecution table that it was not the same prosecutor that was at my trial.

It was also easy to notice that when the judge left his chambers to walk up to the bench, that it was not my trial judge. It was then that I had learned that the judge who oversaw my trial had retired, and the prosecutor from my trial had since left the prosecution office to go into private practice as a defense attorney.

This immediately came to my attention because my appeal lawyer, Mark Zeno, had already advised me that in a 440.10 motion, usually it's the trial judge and the same prosecutor that hears the motion.

I nervously turned to look at my lawyer for reassurance as my mind struggled to adjust to these two curveballs.

No matter, I thought to myself, *I'm confident with the argument that we've prepared.*

Unlike my first trial, where I did not put on a defense because I was so distracted from events that occurred to me which inspired me to become a writer, I was not going to allow that mistake to happen again.

I realized that in order for me to fulfill my destiny I had to show that the two state's witnesses lied. The way it turned out, there was so much overwhelming evidence to show that the state witnesses lied, but also showed that my defense lawyer was responsible for ineffective legal representation.

Throughout all my writing, I have said that I would never use my writing as a platform to proclaim my innocence. Nevertheless, I won the 440.10 motion and had my conviction overturned.

When I heard the words of the judge: "Due to the overwhelming evidence presented from the defense to the court, I'm ruling that your second-degree murder conviction be overturned."

After hearing those words tears began to flow down the side of my face. The very first thought that came to my mind was the power of the energy from the universe that causes our destiny.

I then turned to my lawyer, Mark Zeno, and said, "I tell you in truth, you have no idea on how important of a role you have played in my destiny."

I then asked Mark the question, "When will I be released?" Thinking that I was going to be upset from the answer, Mark hesitated for a moment, before he said, "Don't worry, you're going to be sent back to Clinton, but it will only be for a short time until they do the paperwork for your release."

Not only was I not upset about Mark's answer, despite how bad I hungered for my freedom, but I found some happiness from the thought that I will be able to say good-bye to many of the inmates that I mentor and have become quite fond of.

Even though I could honestly say that I was equally happy for the opportunity to say good-bye and give my best wishes to all the inmates that I have mentored, there was this one inmate in particular that I wanted to say good-bye to more than all the others.

Maybe it was because I found him to be a personal challenge because he was so different than all the rest.

This man called himself Cam, short for Cameron. He was thirty-two years old, tall, lean and muscular, good-looking and white. Immediately I could tell that he was a college graduate with a business degree.

So, he had a head on his shoulders with intelligence, which as one can imagine are two attributes not easily found in an environment like Clinton Prison.

That being said, my first impression of him was that he was a cocky kid with an attitude. To me he was going to be a guy who lived on the periphery of my world: he would do his stint as a porter here on D-block and probably in short order will be chewed up and spit out, then shipped off to a different location than Clinton, which would be fine with me.

Because of the hard environment in prison, Cam stuck out like a sore thumb. You didn't have to be a genius to realize that this kid came from wealth: Early on I was convinced that he ate from a silver spoon and drank from a golden cup.

Being that he was a porter, we interacted here and there and soon despite my initial feelings toward him, we actually became pretty close. Beyond the tough exterior he emitted, there was a guy who was down to earth, thoughtful and even vulnerable.

We did have a few run-ins however, and people who know me know I'm all about respect. That being said, there were a few instances where I thought he was being short with me or perhaps a bit dismissive and I let him have it!

Believe me when I say that I jumped all over him, but you know what? He took it like a man. In fact, it was how he responded to these confrontations that grew the bond between us even more.

So, despite any differences that we might have had, I stuck with him. If the majority of the guys I mentor in Clinton were black or Hispanic, with very little education, no money and from the hood, Cam was the complete opposite.

9

While I truly enjoy helping each and every one of these inmates, Cam's unique circumstances presented a special challenge to me. Frankly, he was a breath of fresh air and I like to think that I finally reached and made a connection with Cam when he sent me this letter:

Uncle Doc,

I want to take a moment and properly express how thankful I am for you getting behind me. To go out of your way and stick your neck out for me is the kindest gesture that I have experienced so far over the course of my two years of being incarcerated.

In the brutally harsh and cold environment that is our world here at Clinton, your act of friendship was something that I haven't experienced in a long time.

Ever since I settled in here next to you, I've increasingly have begun to believe in myself and my ability to succeed in my war against all of the negative forces that constantly confront one in a place like this.

Over the past two years, I have experienced many long-term periods of depression, where I would sit on my bunk, staring into nothingness and frankly feeling sorry for myself.

I allowed negative thoughts to break me down and completely disable me for months at a time. I allowed week upon week to pass without picking up a book, writing in my journal or even showering!

But ever since we met, you welcomed me with open arms and whether you knew it or not, immediately began pouring a much-needed dose of positivity into my life.

In turn, I haven't experienced any sort of behavior like that ever becoming your neighbor. As you've mentioned to me, with the way I am and how I carry myself, (something that I will work on because of your feedback) you probably haven't sensed how thankful I am and what a great impact being around you has had on me.

I take everything you say to heart, Doc, I will forever cherish our bond, something I'll never stop working on, and friendship for the rest of my life.

They might succeed in getting me moved to another block, but you will always be a part of my life (in and out of prison) and I will never lose touch/contact with you.

There's so much more I want to say and express to you, but whenever I reach down deep like this, I always have trouble putting my feelings and thoughts into words.

I imagine tomorrow I'll wake up clear-headed and will probably want to expand on my sentiment here. Sleep well tonight Doc, see you in the morning.

Yours,

Cameron

Throughout the years of mentoring so many of the inmates, I have received many letters from inmates expressing their gratitude for the time that I had spent with them.

To me, there is no greater reward than to know that someone is expressing their appreciation that you have helped them in their life.

The time finally came when my name was called on the PA system telling me to report to the bubble. When I arrived, officer Schnider had a big grin on his face when he said, "Doc, you're being released at 9:00 a.m. tomorrow.

My first thought after hearing the good news was to go to the phone and call my friend, Tommy Ciardella. He had offered to send his limo driver to pick me up.

When the next morning arrived, I said to myself, "*The last chapter of my life begins today.*" I knew I was ready both physically and mentally to go out into the world to continue my journey to destiny.

To my surprise, when I walked out the doors to the opposite side of that humongous wall my legs began to tremble like they were silly putty. I was completely shocked by how my emotions completely took over my body.

As I took my first steps as a free man, I was mesmerized by the sun's glare and all the bright colors of nature. For the past seven years I lived in a box dominated by dull greens, black, and every variation of gray you can imagine.

When I exited the gate, it felt as if I entered into the new world, as if I stepped into the page of a coloring book.

Then I began to think about what I was going to eat for my first meal. As if someone had just turned on a faucet, my mouth began to salivate. My mind was running wild, conjuring up images of my all-time favorite foods.

Should I grab a pizza at the local Italian joint that the CO's are always going on about? Or maybe some greasy Chinese food that I love so much? Perhaps a large juicy T-bone steak or maybe a thick veal chop with hot peppers? Maybe Dannemora has an imported Italian specialty store where I can create my own authentic Italian sub-sandwich.

The way it turned out, being unable to choose what food I was going to eat first didn't matter. To my surprise, I was unable to eat, these desires faded as I quickly realized that I had absolutely no appetite.

As a deep thinker, I really found it interesting that although I had my shit together both physically, spiritually and emotionally, subconsciously I was overwhelmed by my emotions from the thought of having my freedom.

As I rode in the limo that was headed to my home, each hour of the six-hour trip I waited for my appetite to come back, but that time never came.

As I sat in the back of the limo all sprawled out with no energy, I was puzzled why I was not experiencing joy and excitement. I then started to search for the answer as I went into my deep-thinking mode, I found myself becoming confused.

I then started to reminisce on the story that the CO's had told me about how the prison investigator was searching for some kind of an answer to how the prison bars got bent.

I then began to profusely sweat as it came back to my memory that it was I who held onto those bars on the gate of D-block, as two of those inmates jumped onto my back.

I then asked myself the question, *"Could it have been me who bent those bars?"* I then started to get nervous and more confused as I said to myself, *"I can't tell anyone about this, people will really think I'm nuts."*

When I arrived in my hometown the limo driver dropped me off at my youngest son, Brian's house. I was going to stay in his guest room until I could find a condo to buy.

When I went to prison, I was living with my soulmate in her home, but sadly, years away from each other had grown us apart.

As I opened the door to enter my son's home the first people to greet me were Gina and Luke, two of my precious grandchildren.

As I began to hug and kiss the two kids that I left seven years ago, I now find them both to be grown-up teenagers.

Suddenly the emotions that I had been suppressing, since exiting those towering walls of the "House of Horrors" overcame me, as tears began to trickle down my cheeks.

I then began to be hugged by my daughter-in-law, Amy and my son, Brian. They then told me that knowing what time I was going to arrive, they instructed family and friends to wait a few hours before they come over to see you so you have time to settle down.

When I walked into the dining room, I was truly touched by what I saw on the table. Amy made trays of my father's famous chicken savoy and pasta fagioli. She even made my special creation, chicken pepperoni.

I was always proud of Amy not only for being a great wife and mother but also because she tried so hard to learn special new recipes so she could cook them for family.

Shockingly to everyone including myself, I was unable to eat anything. My appetite still had not yet returned. Even though that was puzzling to me, more important to me was that I let Amy know how appreciative I was for all the hard work she put into cooking those special meals for me.

I then went into the living room and turned the giant screen TV on and then went to sit on the reclining lounge chair. When I woke-up my son told me that it was only minutes after I sat down in that chair before I was sawing wood.

By the time it took me to fully awaken, family and friends were starting to come in to welcome me back to the real world. As happy as I was to see everyone, I was lethargic and still had no energy.

All of the people in my life, particularly those closest to me, know me to have a big personality, so my calm and tranquil state puzzled me and as well as my family.

Is this the new me? I thought nervously, *what happened to the person with the tremendous will and drive? Will I be able to fulfill my destiny if I continue on like this?*

That question was answered the next morning when I woke up with enough energy to move a mountain. The first thing I had on my agenda was to join a physical fitness center.

Ironically, the fitness center that I chose to join was at one time a competitor to the fitness centers that my brother and I owned.

ᓚᓂᓂ Chapter Two ᓂᓂᓚ

My plan was to put every ounce of energy that I could muster into spreading the message from "Beyond the Beyond" and I was convinced that I'd have to be in peak shape in order to be successful in all my writing and public speaking endeavors.

My insight tells me that this journey ahead of me wasn't going to be a walk in the park, so I had to get started immediately. I noticed yesterday how my emotions had an intense effect on my body and my abilities.

The phenomena that ensued were nothing short of incredible, however completely unexplainable! So, my gut tells me that if I'm going to keep my path toward destiny on track, I'd have to keep my emotions in check.

Little did I know after having that thought what was about to shortly take place.

Here I was having my first workout with weights in some time. Of course, with my expertise in physical fitness bodybuilding and weightlifting, I knew it would be better to start off extremely slow until I gradually started to get back into condition.

It was at this time that an incredible event took place. I had just completed a set of shoulder presses with eighty pounds on the weightlifting machine. At that moment, as I was going over to the bench press area of the machine, a song that was special to me was playing over the sound system.

It really started to affect my emotions; I was feeling very nostalgic as a flood of emotions began to run through me.

Assuming that the pin was in the one-hundred-pound slot, I began to pump out ten reps on the bench press.

To my shocking surprise, after doing ten reps I discovered that the pin was in the 1,000-pound slot.

My first thought was there is some kind of a mistake, the machine must be broken, no mortal man could do a 1,000-pound bench press one time, not to mention ten times.

I then went to the few members that were in the area at the time I was on the bench press machine to see if they saw me doing the lift. They all had the same response, "We didn't notice."

My heart started to beat fast as I searched for an explanation. I then walked back to the bench press machine, checked that the pin was in the same spot, showing the number of 1,000.

I then laid back down onto the bench press machine and attempted to do the lift. I was unable to move the bar not even a fraction of an inch.

What the hell is going on here; was I losing my mind? My heart began to flutter, could all that time I spent behind bars messed with my psyche?

Searching for an explanation, I recalled that strange instance where I bent those prison bars with my bare hands.

Remembering the situation, I was walking down the tier when I was caught off guard and jumped by those hoodlums. They came out of nowhere; though I remember how quickly I snapped into battle mode and how fiercely I fought back in order to defend myself.

What little punks! I took care of these guys with an occasional home-cooked meal and even spent time with them, trying to help them work through problems and impart some of my wisdom and this is how they thank me?

Just as it did when the incident occurred, this betrayal got under my skin and really irked the hell out of me. Just thinking about these ungrateful thugs had my heart racing and my emotions flustered, and then BOOM!

It hit me like a ton of bricks, my emotions, that's it! That's the common denominator behind these instances that led me to exhibit such supernatural strength.

Just prior to each act I can remember this significantly heightened sense of emotion and excitement accompanied by the feeling of my heart beating out of my chest.

If this revelation turns out to be true, I'm going to have to learn how to keep my emotions in check. I thought again about how I snapped my assailants' bones like twigs and it began to set in how incredible this new found power of mine really was. And on top of that, how dangerous and unpredictable it was.

Before I went any further in contemplating any possibilities and potential benefits of my having this new found hulk-like strength, I came to grips with how important it would be for me to keep all of this on the down-low.

I mean what would happen if my friends and family got wind of all of this? Wouldn't they think that I was some kind of freak?

In the next few days, I had made arrangements to meet with the people who now run my hometown and the high school that I attended.

Bobby G. was now the mayor and Chizzie Vuono was the President of the Board of Education. We have been close friends ever since we played high school football together.

My purpose for meeting with them at that particular time was to see if they were able to get approval from the town council and the Board of Education for me to speak to the students of Lyndhurst High School.

Minutes before I was about to be introduced to a crowd of over 1,000 students, I started to get a little nervous. This was going to be the first time I was going to be speaking in front of a large group since my incarceration.

As Chizzie and I were sitting in the Athletic Director's office reminiscing about our high school days, a teacher came into the office to inform me that I was about to be introduced.

When I walked into the hallway I could hear the voice of my dear friend, Mayor Robert Giangeruso speaking on the microphone. He said, "Students of Lyndhurst High, I would like to introduce to you, bestselling author, Paul "Doc" Gaccione, better known in this area from years past as "TR" Gaccione.

As I entered the gym, I was being applauded by over 1,000 students as I walked to the podium that was placed in the center of the basketball court.

The first thing that I said to the audience was, "The last time I spoke at this podium in the middle of the basketball court was to the students of fifty-five years ago."

I was the captain of the football team who had not played a single game the entire season. We were having a football rally for the last football game of the season. My leg was still stiff from the surgery after having a football injury before the first game of the season.

I did let the audience know that I took my frustrations out by motivating myself to recuperate my knee and then get into shape to win the New Jersey State Boxing Championship on TV before the school year ended.

I then let the students know that being on this basketball court reminded me of a story that took place when I was a freshman here at LHS, almost sixty years ago.

The story takes place on this court during the middle of a basketball game that both Mayor Bobby G. and I were playing in. It was the middle of the second quarter and as the action was going on, Sam Ferrara, the woodshop teacher, walked into the court and grabbed our beloved Mayor by the ear and escorted him off the court and back to the classroom to serve detention.

To this day, the Mayor claims that he had forgotten that he had detention that day.

That story brought much laughter from the crowd. It had also brought much laughter through all those years to both Bobby G. and me.

As I began to speak to the students about my message, I first made them aware of the special gift that is given to all of us, and that is our imagination. I let them know that they should never allow anyone to tamper with it, "It's yours and only yours."

I made them aware that anything that they are capable of imagining, as long as what they are imagining feels natural to them, it is obtainable.

I use the analogy if you were imagining playing tackle for the New York Giants, does that feel natural to you, certainly not. You're not six foot five inches tall, 350 pounds, but let's say that you were imagining writing a book, does that feel natural? Certainly yes, all you need to get started is a piece of paper and a pen.

I then let the students know that the greatest secret to achieving success and happiness in life is to always be positive. It's so important to know that positivity will always defeat negativity.

When I began speaking about destiny and people being a product of their environment, I wanted to elaborate on those subjects. I then used the President of the Board of Education, Mr. James Vuono, better known by friends as "Chizzie" to be my example.

I then told the students that right before the beginning of Mr. Vuono's high school sophomore year, he was very close to quitting school. It was only after his father came to me and his son's other close friends like Mayor Bobby G. that we talked him into staying in school.

Not only was Mr. Vuono a good football player, his close friends were also good football players. Being a product of his environment, if Mr. Vuono's friends were not playing football and all quitting school, the odds would have been great that Mr. Vuono's destiny would have been much different.

The way his destiny turned out, he became a great football player who graduated from both high school and college. He then went on to become a high school teacher and football coach for over thirty years.

The point I want to make is that if Mr. Vuono was the product of a different environment, most likely the road of his destiny would have turned out different.

I then made the students aware that there are techniques to be able to self-motivate and the importance of this technique is because we are all vulnerable to fall into depression or a rut from time to time.

Of course, I gave them Doc's five ingredients to success: purpose, imagination, determination, confidence, and attitude.

It was then that I began to become emotional as I gave the students the message that I received from "Beyond the Beyond." We are accountable for our actions here on earth, and by our efforts and actions each and every day we are able to influence our destiny.

This is the message I will spend the rest of my life spreading to the masses of people.

As I said those words, I started to become extremely emotional. I felt such an incredible amount of energy building within my body that I feared an explosion similar to the Big Bang.

And then it happened, I struck the podium with my fist with such force that the heavy-duty sturdy podium completely fell apart.

The audience was in utter shock at what they witnessed; even my friends couldn't believe their eyes.

I tried to cover-up what I had done by saying, "The podium must be really old, it looks like the same one I used fifty-five years ago." That statement brought laughter from the crowd.

The final statement I made brought joy to the crowd when I said that each of the students was going to receive all four of my books.

After leaving the gym to a standing ovation, Bobby G., Chizzie, and I went out to lunch. I could tell that both of them were quite pleased with how the morning went.

I guess they were relieved that the stories I chose to tell about them were not of their real mischievous nature.

When I went back to the house I laid down on the bed and I began to think of how my fist was able to destroy a very sturdy podium, that one swing with a heavy-duty sledgehammer would not have been able to destroy.

As I continued to think about what took place, I was now convinced that this supernatural strength was entering my body whenever I was getting extremely emotional.

When the next morning arrived, I had a 10 o'clock appointment with an old high school friend, Rich LaManna. He was retired after serving as a high school principal for the last twenty-five years.

After reading all of the four books that I had authored, Rich suggested that he would like to volunteer to be my publicist. He expressed to me that he believed in the message that I was trying to convey to the masses of people.

Wow! I was overwhelmed by his suggestion. I said to myself, *I could use him to get me speaking engagements in the college circuit.* It was then that I realized that he could also do that in the prison system and even with major club organizations.

It only took Rich a few days before he had me scheduled to speak to a group of inmates at the Bergen County jail in New Jersey. When I went to speak, I was anticipating a group of at least 300 inmates, so when I was introduced and noticed that the audience fell short of a count of fifty, I was disappointed.

Nevertheless, I spoke with enthusiasm and conviction as if I was speaking in front of a crowd of 100,000 strong.

The next day Rich had me speaking in front of forty aging, wealthy silver foxes. They were all literary intellectuals who belonged to a book club from the hotsy-totsy affluent area of upper Bergen County in New Jersey.

When I was introduced, I walked from the back of this large room through an aisle that had approximately twenty-five fully cushioned leather folding chairs on both sides of the aisle.

After I reached the front of the room, I approached a small one-foot high platform, after stepping up I noticed that there was a microphone attached to the podium.

As I gazed out into the audience, I couldn't help but notice how many women were sporting blue-gray hairdos. I also couldn't help notice despite their casual dress wear, how extremely elegant they all appeared.

I'm sure that one would say that all the BLING that they had on display helped me to form my opinion.

Before I began to speak, I found myself nervous and intimidated from the thought that this would be the first time that I would be speaking in front of a group of literary silver foxes.

As I grabbed the neck of the microphone my instinct told me to just be the man that I am. So, I started to speak by saying, "Distinguished ladies, I hope you didn't come to see some special literary writer, for I am a man who struggles with his own vocabulary."

That statement brought a good laugh and not a sarcastic laugh from the ladies.

I then went on to say that life sometimes has some people experience choices that give twists and turns in their life they would have never expected to ever occur, which completely turns the road to their destiny in a completely different direction.

"You see ladies, there is no doubt that I am one of those people. I say this because I did not choose writing, writing chose me."

I only write when I'm inspired to write and then the words just come to me. The only reason I write is to bring forth a message, but I do try my very best to entertain the reader at the same time.

The speaking engagement with the ladies of the book club turned out to go very well. The way that things turned out was the women were very receptive to me for my candor and for not pretending to be a literary man.

The feedback that I also received from the ladies was that they were appreciative and inspired by the message I brought forth to them.

The next day when I met with my new publicist, Rich LaManna, I informed him that both speaking engagements that he arranged for me, the prison and the book club, went very well. I also let him know how appreciative I was for the job he did making those arrangements.

I then told Rich, "Here is my dilemma, my insight is telling me that I need to be speaking in the presence of much larger numbers. Speaking to an audience of forty or fifty people is not going to be the pace I need to be on to fulfill my mission."

Rich replied, Doc, to be honest with you, in the short time that I have been spending on trying to set up speaking engagements for you, I have noticed that it's difficult to arrange speaking engagements to large audiences without name recognition.

Rich went on to say, Doc, despite your accomplishment of penning four books, you still have not yet reached that plateau of drawing people.

I responded to Richie's comment by agreeing with him. I told him I realize that name recognition was important for an opportunity to speak to a large audience.

I had then noticed that Rich was pleased that I was able to see the dilemma that he was facing when he was trying to set up large speaking engagements for me.

Here is what I told Rich, "I tell you in truth, ever since I have been inspired to bring forth the message from "Beyond the Beyond," I have been given the insight on how to continue my mission."

I then told Rich that I would like to sleep on the situation, and if it's destined to be, I will come up with the answer. I then told him that I'd meet with him tomorrow.

After I left Rich, I went to take a walk in the park. As I was walking, I was saying to myself, *I must find a way to get publicity.*

Later I went to sit on a park bench as I began to meditate. As I'm in deep thought, I ask my mother's spirit for a sign. It was then that I started to recollect how recently I was given this unexplainable super incredible strength each time I became emotional.

After having that thought, this weird feeling entered my body, I began to shake. It felt like it was an electrical current, it started in my head and went through my body to my toes. I never had an experience like that ever before.

It was then that I was able to see that I was being given this incredible strength for a purpose. My insight was telling me that I could use this special power that was being given to me so that I could achieve the publicity needed to fulfill my mission.

My first thought was I could break some weight-lifting records. WOW! At my age, that should give me some worldwide publicity.

Even though at first I thought that was a great idea, my insight was telling me that was not the answer.

I then started to think back to my early days as a youngster, and how I always fantasized about becoming the heavyweight boxing champion of the world.

My mind then immediately shifted over to when I was jumped by those three young tough guys in prison, and how I single-handedly destroyed all three of them.

I then told myself, *WOW! I did this as an overweight, out of shape, seventy-two-year-old man. I then started to reflect back on the reaction of all the correctional officers that heard about that event.*

I then began to refresh my memory on how much attention and publicity that situation received.

Now my crazy mind was starting to get excited, I said to myself, *Oh my God, with this special unexplainable strength that has been given to me, I could win the heavyweight championship of the world.*

If I was ever able to accomplish this feat, I would be receiving all the publicity that I could ever want or imagine for my mission.

As my mind continued to race with many thoughts, I said to myself, *As I'm winning my fights, once the news media takes notice, they will have an interest in my story. I will then be getting enormous publicity, which would allow me to start doing my public speaking to large crowds.*

Now that I was through fantasizing, I asked myself the question, *How could I tell anyone what I'm thinking? My family will admit me to a psych ward!*

I didn't want to let anyone know about this supernatural strength that was coming into my body. I wasn't even sure if that strength would ever come back.

My next thought was if I attempted to go ahead with that plan, it would be stopped because no state boxing commission would ever give a seventy-two-year-old man a boxing license.

That last thought started to smother the excitement that I was starting to have of becoming the world's heavyweight champion.

My other situation was that I still couldn't even guarantee myself that I would receive that super strength each time that my emotions are stirred up.

When the mail was delivered that day, I received a letter from Sophia, my thirteen-year-old granddaughter. Now that I'm home from prison after seven years, I'm hoping that I can become close to my children and grandkids.

As I opened the envelope, I began to read the letter:

Dear Grandpa Doc,

Happy Birthday! I heard you're turning seventy-two. My dad was telling me stories about you and how you loved these frozen drinks from New York City and how you would have parties at your house and have huge amounts of these frozen drinks. The last memory I have of you is when we went to the Cheesecake Factory.

I think I was about six or seven. Right now I'm twelve turning thirteen on August 30th. I am reading your first book, I just started reading it and it's pretty good so far.

I think I took on some of your qualities, I am a writer/poet and one of my poems is published in a book. They said I would make a great author for writing stories and being a poet.

Writing poems just came easy to me, you should try it, and it takes away the stress and anxiety. Especially for me, if you haven't heard, my mom and dad are splitting up, but we'll all be okay. I hope you're doing well. I think I'll write more letters to you and maybe they will be a lot neater. I hope you write back soon.

Love,

Your granddaughter,

Sophia Gaccione

When I began to read Sophia's letter, I started to become teary-eyed, as I continued on the tears began to flow down the side of my face.

After reading her letter there was now a poem that she had sent to me that she wrote. I was completely overwhelmed as I began to read the poem.

Took less than a year for the world I know to be turned around up and down and inside out. Mom and Dad getting divorced just because it got worse.

It's hard but I'll get through it, it's a matter of time before you all know it.

Distracting and relaxing, writing and sighing, it's all just because of the matter of the timing.

Moving out, coming in, it's just a matter of fitting in.

It's all okay, I'll get through it, but I need some support are you up to it?

Gets hard and lonely and I don't want to feel alone in this world that I've always known.

Life gets tough especially when you try to deal with the grownup stuff.

It's hard to add when you're busy subtracting.

Does it ever get easier when you're multiplying or dividing?

Like a puzzle taken apart with a missing piece it's easier to try to find it then just give up on it.

~By Sophia Gaccione

After reading that poem, words could not truly express the love that I was feeling. As the tears continued to flow, I said to myself, *I only wish I could hug that little creature at this moment and tell her how much I love her.*

When I thought how hard I would hug and squeeze her if she was here, that is when I realized how emotional I was getting. I then started to see how this little girl was stirring up my feelings and emotions to a point that I could actually feel this incredible strength entering my body.

At that moment I got off the chair I was sitting on and rushed through the house and out the front door. Without hesitation, I then went to my son's brand new 2020 Rover truck that was parked in the driveway.

I went to the front of the truck, put my hands under the bumper, and started to repeatedly lift the front end of the truck up and down as I was chanting to myself, Sophia, Sophia, Sophia.

There it was, I then realized that unquestionably each time my emotions are stirred-up, this super strength enters my body, and I am now totally convinced.

Now that I'm reassured that each time my emotions are stirred-up this super strength enters my body; I'm going to call Rich to meet with me tomorrow morning.

In one breath as excited as I am to tell him my plan, in another breath I'm concerned that Rich is going to really think I'm nuts.

Rich was punctual meeting with me at 10:00 a.m. sharp at the Lyndhurst Diner. After having some small talk and our first cup of coffee, I broke the news to Rich of my plan.

I told him that after leaving him yesterday, I went to the park to meditate, during this time insight was given to me. I then asked Rich, "Knowing that you read all four of my books, do you believe when I say that I receive insight?"

Rich replied, "Doc, despite that I was looking to fill some of the void now that I'm retired when you offered me the opportunity to be part of your mission, I became overwhelmed with joy."

"Doc, I believe so strong in the road to your destiny."

That is when I said to Rich, "I'm happy to hear your answer. Now you might think I'm nuts when I tell you that my insight is telling me to go back into the boxing ring."

I can get the publicity needed for me to get great name recognition so I can draw large crowds to hear me speak.

Rich responded after almost choking on his bacon and cheese omelet when he said, "Doc, I know that fifty years ago you were one of the toughest around, but that was fifty years ago, you're now a seventy-two-year-old man."

My response to Rich was my insight has not failed me as of yet, and for that reason, I must follow my destiny.

Rich responded, "I believe in your insight, I believe in your mission, and I also believe that you're nuts, but you have my support and loyalty."

After we completed our breakfast, we made arrangements to meet the next day to start my plan. I then told Rich that I was going to ask two of my close friends, Johnny Luzzi and Tommy Ciardella, to meet with us.

Rich replied, "Two great guys, haven't seen either one in a while, I'll look forward to seeing them." After Rich and I parted, I began to make arrangements to meet with Tommy and Luzzi tomorrow.

Neither one had their cell phones on, so I left a message for the two of them to meet with me at 10:00 o'clock tomorrow morning at the Lyndhurst Diner.

I told them to only call me back if they were unable to make the appointment to meet for breakfast. Knowing that both of them had just recently retired, I was quite confident that they both would show up. I was happy to notice that neither one of them called me back through the night.

ᏨᎯᏌᏧᏂᎯᏂᏧᏂ Chapter Three ᏧᏂᏧᏂ

W hen the next morning arrived, I left early to get to the diner to make sure that we had a table of four available before the guys arrived. Call it a coincidence they all pulled up at the same time.

After the hugs that Rich was giving to Luzzi and Tommy for not seeing them in many years, we all sat and started to shoot the breeze as we were having our first cup of Joe.

It was then that I began to explain to the guys my plan about going into the ring. The first response came from Tommy when he asked me the question, "Are you freaking nuts?"

Luzzi then chimed in by saying, "Why are you doing this, is it money you need?" Tommy then asked, "Money you need, how much?"

I replied to both of them, "I don't need money, you both know that I don't care about money." After making that statement, I then hesitated, thought for a second and then turned to Rich and said, "WOW!" Rich, I haven't even thought about the money that could be earned from my plan."

I then said to Rich, "That money could be put toward the expenses of the mission."

At this point in the conversation, Tom and Luz were completely lost. That's when I turned to both of them and said, "I need you both to be my co-managers and trainers for my new pro-boxing career. Rich is going to be my publicist."

That's when Tommy turned to Richie with puzzlement on his face as he asked him the question, "Is he serious, or is this nut kidding?"

With a grin on his face, Rich replied to Tommy's question, "Tom, he's not kidding." Luzzi started to laugh as he said, "Doc, I'm sure happy to see that the time you spent in prison hasn't affected your brain."

Well! All four of us started to laugh hysterically at Luzzi's sarcastic comment.

After we all regained our composure, I said to the guys in a stern tone of voice, "Trust me, I know what I'm doing, I'm going to take you guys on a journey that you'll never forget."

Tommy then said, "Doc, you know we're here for you if you really need us, but my question to you is what the hell are we going to do as your manager and your trainer, we don't know anything about the fight game."

I responded to Tommy's doubt by assuring him not to worry, I will be showing him and Luzzi all that they will need to know.

Luzzi then responded by saying, "If I'm your trainer, I could sprinkle some cocaine into your smelling salt bottle in between rounds that should give you some extra energy." We all started laughing again from Luzzi's comment.

John then said, "All kidding aside, you could get killed doing something as crazy as that." I responded, "Luz, you know me for sixty years, you know I'm going to do this."

Luz, I know that you and Tommy LACK THE EXPERIENCE to take on an endeavor such as this, but my insight is telling me that I want you two to take the journey.

Tommy then busted out laughing; I turned to him and said, "What's so funny?"

He replied, "I started to think about the story you told in your first book, "Beyond the Beyond."

You were at the heavyweight champion Floyd Paterson's house having lunch with him and his lawyer. You were trying to put together the National Boxing League that you created back then.

You then began to tell Floyd and his lawyer the story of how the boxing trainer was trying to motivate his fighter in between the rounds during a fight.

Tommy went on to complete the story by saying that in the very first round, the fighter is getting his ass kicked, his lip was split, and blood was flowing. When the bell rang for the one-minute rest, the trainer is telling his fighter that he's doing a great job and for him to keep up the good work.

In the second round, he's getting the shit kicked out of him again. His face is all busted up and covered with blood.

At the end of the second round, again the trainer starts telling his fighter how great a job he's doing, and that he should keep up the good work.

When the bell is getting ready to ring for the start of the third round, the fighter turns to his trainer and says, "Do me a favor, keep an eye out for the referee, because somebody is punching the shit out of me."

As we were all still laughing the waitress came over to our table to take our order. My mouth started to salivate when I heard the guys ordering pancakes, omelets and side orders of home fries, bacon and ham with extra toast and whipped butter.

When the waitress turned to me, I told her that I would like a fruit cup and a glass of skim milk. Hearing those words startled Tommy and Luzzi. Tommy then turned to Richie and said, "I can't believe my ears, here is a guy with the biggest appetite that I have ever seen and he's ordering a fruit cup.

I replied, "I'm 280 pounds, the heaviest that I have ever been. I have to start to get into shape and lose sixty pounds."

Luzzi responded to my comment by saying, "Doc, your entire body looks like it's still all muscle, it's just your fat belly where you have to lose the sixty pounds."

Hearing Johnny's observation, I turned to Tommy and said with some sarcasm in my voice, "See Tom, Luzzi is a genius, and you were worried that you and Luzzi weren't qualified to be my manager and trainer." Again everyone started laughing.

Luz then said with enthusiasm in his voice, "I have another observation, if Doc could go through this entire meal by just eating a fruit cup, how could we not take him seriously," again everyone started to laugh.

After everyone completed their breakfast, I asked Tommy and Luzzi the question, "I need to know right now, are you on board with me? I promise you that I know what I'm doing."

Tommy then looked at Luzzi who was shaking his head up and down. Tommy then turned to me and said, "We're both with you, you sick jerk."

I then said to the guys in a stern voice, we start tomorrow. I then turned to Richie and said, "As I'm getting into shape and Tommy, Luzzi, and I are working on a game plan, I need you to continue to arrange speaking engagements for me regardless of how small they are."

I then turned to Tommy and John and asked them if they were able to meet with me every morning during the week at 9:00 o'clock for the next few weeks?

After they both committed to me, I told them we will meet across the street from the Lyndhurst Diner at the King's Court Racquetball and Physical Fitness Center each day. I told them that I had just become a member and they have a nice lounge area where we could have our meetings.

This will work out perfectly because each day after our meeting, I will be able to do my training.

As we were getting ready to leave the diner, I told Rich to reach out to me immediately as soon as he arranges a speaking engagement for me, I then told the other guys that I would see them tomorrow morning at nine across the street.

After leaving the Lyndhurst Diner, I was proceeding to Highway Route 3 which then turns into Highway Route 46. I was looking to get to the Olympia Diner, which was located on Route 46 in Wayne, New Jersey.

I was going there to meet Angie, an old soulmate of mine from years gone by. As I'm driving, it seemed to be only a minute since Route 3 turned into Route 46 when I saw an overturned truck on the opposite side of the highway.

I felt a deep twinge in my chest, thinking about the possible injuries that could result from such a devastating accident. I thought of my friend who was involved in a scene similar to this, a run-in with a drunk driver on his way home from football practice.

Once a top college recruited prospect and now paralyzed from the waist down.

Immediately, I pulled my son's Rover onto the grass that made up the center median, jumped out of the Rover and ran toward the overturned truck.

There was a Good Samaritan already on the scene and as I got closer, I overheard his panicked conversation with the 911 operator: he was telling that the man was ejected and now is trapped underneath the weight of the truck!

"I tried to pull him free, but his legs are pinned down and his chest is being crushed by the truck's door; hurry, please, I'm afraid he won't make it much longer!"

When I approached the overturned truck, I had a heavy heart, the scene of my friend's accident and the devastating consequences occupying my mind. As I bent down to grab hold of the truck, I felt like I was almost in a dreamlike state.

In my imagination, I pictured my friend under that truck and as a tear rolled down my cheek, I felt a surge of energy, almost like electricity pulsing through my veins.

I closed my eyes and let out a roar of a breath, as I shot out of my crouch with all the might that I could possibly muster. All I could hear was the scraping of metal while the truck's cab lifted up, followed by the compression of springs as the weight of the truck settled back onto its wheels again.

I then ran over to the other guy that was trying to help, he shouted out to me, "the pressure is off his chest, he's able to breathe, he's going to live."

He then said, "Who are you, how did you do that?" As he was in awe of what he witnessed, and as he was asking those questions, I heard the sound of sirens from afar.

That's when I started to panic and ran to my truck and took off. My heart was pounding as I was headed to meet Angie. I was really nervous that someone would find out about my secret.

When I arrived at the diner, I tried to get my composure before I entered. When I went through the door, Angie was sitting at the first table.

The first words out of her mouth were, "You're always late, you haven't changed."

I responded, "Honey, you should only know what I've been through."

She responded, "Don't you honey me."

Angie then said, "You haven't changed, you're always doing something exciting, whose life did you save today?" We both then started laughing, she should only know.

Angie and I spent over an hour talking and catching up with our lives. I was so happy to hear that she's doing well, that means so much to me because I will always have love for her.

After I left Angie and was driving back to my son Brian's house, I started to reflect on what occurred earlier. My first thought was how thankful I was for being able to save that truck driver's life before I then started to get a concern that someone might discover my secret.

When the evening news went on, I almost swallowed my dentures. They were talking about the accident that occurred this morning on Route 46 when the truck overturned.

Then to my surprise, they were interviewing the man that was helping the truck driver. He was explaining how the truck driver was lodged in the wreck where he was unable to breathe, his chest was being crushed, and he was going to die.

"Then out of nowhere this old man comes and turns the truck right side up, which saved the man's life."

Now everyone is looking for this mysterious old superman. The next morning all the major TV news channels were telling the story about the mysterious old superman.

All the major New Jersey and New York newspapers had front-page coverage of the mysterious missing superman ghost.

The next morning, I left a little early to meet the guys for our meeting at the King's Court. When I walked into the lounge area, I was immediately reminded of yesterday's activities when I overheard two women talking about the mysterious missing ghost.

When the guys arrived, the first question that I asked Tommy was, "Did your limo driver bring you here?" When he replied, "Yes" I responded, "Good," you, Luzzi and I are going to Trenton, New Jersey to the office of the Boxing Commission; we're going there so I can apply for a boxing license."

It's a two-hour drive. While driving in the limo, Luzzi brought up yesterday's news when he said, "Did you guys hear on the news that a man is claiming that a mysterious old man came on the scene of an accident and uprighted an overturned truck?"

Tommy started laughing as he said, "Luz, that's the kind of strength that Doc is going to need to have a chance in the ring." All three of us laughed at that comment.

Before we arrived at our destination, I prepared Tommy ahead of time for when we would go into the Boxing Commission office. I told him that if at any time someone was giving me a hard time or objecting to my request, I want you to simply say, I'm going to have my lawyer sue the New Jersey Boxing Commission and the State of New Jersey for depriving my fighter the right to make a living.

When we arrived at Trenton, after locating the building that houses the State Boxing Commission office, as we entered this large open room, we saw this long counter. Behind the counter was a large space that had six people sitting at desks, behind that appeared to be a private office which I assumed to be the boxing commissioner's office.

As we approached the counter, three over seventy-year-old men, there was this heavy-set black woman standing there. She then politely asked us, "Can I help you, gentlemen?" I replied, "Yes please, we're here to obtain one boxing license."

The woman responded by saying to me, "Sugar, you have to bring your fighter with you, he has to fill out the forms and sign them in person."

I then responded with a slight grin, "Here I am, yours truly."

You had to see the look on the woman's face when she said, "Lordy, Lordy, what you talking about old man?" That remark started Tommy and Luzzi laughing.

My response was, "Yes I would personally like to get a boxing license, I'm going back into the ring." She then came back at me, "Lord Jesus, sugar, have you lost your mind?"

The counter woman then turned to the woman that was sitting at the closest desk and said, "Jo, this old man wants to be a fighter." JoJo then got up from her desk and walked over to me, after she looked me over from head to toe, she said, "Sweetie, you don't want to be a fighter, I'm going to make a lover out of you."

The people sitting at the other five desks couldn't help but overhear the entire conversation, so they all stood up in front of their desks to get a better look at me as it appeared they were trying to hold back the laughter.

JoJo then turned to the counter lady and said, "Beverly, you can't give this crazy man a license," that's when I kicked Tommy in the shin and then he immediately said, "If you don't give my fighter the license, I'm going to sue the New Jersey Boxing Commission and the State of New Jersey for depriving my fighter the right to make a living."

When Beverly heard that threat, she had a concern, so she decided not to decide on her own. So, she picked up the phone and asked for the deputy commissioner, a moment later, this man walked out of the office I assumed was the commissioner's office.

He walked over to the counter and introduced himself as Mr. Thompson, deputy commissioner. He then asked, "How can I help you gentlemen?"

Beverly responded by saying as she was pointing toward me, "This seventy-two-year-old man would like a boxing license to fight in the ring."

Mr. Thompson responded by saying, "You can't be serious, one of the greatest heavyweight champs ever, George

Foreman, when he came out of retirement at the age of fifty-two was crazy, and he was the strongest and hardest puncher ever."

This time Tommy didn't wait to respond when he said to the department, "If you don't issue my fighter a license, I'm going to sue you, the Boxing Commission, and the State of New Jersey for depriving my fighter the right to make a living."

Luzzi then for the first time chimed in when he said to Mr. Thompson, "Sir, I'm an expert on lawsuits, you're going to lose so much money that the State of New Jersey is going to have to close down the Boxing Commission office, they will not be able to afford to keep it running, you all will be out of a job."

Would you believe it was what Luzzi said that scared the hell out of Mr. Thompson, and made him say, "What the hell, Beverly, issue him a boxing license, he's going to have to pass the physical the day of the fight anyway."

Before Luzzi made that statement, he wasn't even paying attention. Here is what happened, as everything was going on, another woman from her desk walked over to Luzzi and started to come on to him, she appeared to be in her mid-forties and was a real looker. She had a figure and a face that you couldn't take your eyes off.

It turned out that this woman was attracted to Luzzi and his hair plugs, hip replacement, and store-bought suntan. Since grammar school, he's always been getting the girls.

Fortunately, he paid attention to what was going on at the right time to make that statement.

As we were walking out of the boxing office, each one of us was struggling to make the effort not to laugh. When we entered into the limo to head back to North Jersey, we couldn't hold it in any longer as we all burst into laughter.

During the time that we were still hysterically laughing, the limo driver said to Tommy, "it appears like you fellows had a real good time." As Tommy was still laughing, he answered his driver, "These guys are completely nuts."

Tom then said to me, "What you told me to say worked out perfect, and then to see what Luzzi said, put the cherry on the cake." I then responded to both of them by saying, "DESTINY my good fellows, DESTINY."

Tommy then came back at me, "Was it destiny that Luzzi could have gotten laid?" We all started laughing again.

When we returned from our trip before we parted, I told Tommy and Luzzi, "Good job men, we're off and running now that we have obtained the boxing license, I'll see you guys 9:00 tomorrow morning."

The first thing that I did when I got to my son Brian's house was to call Richie. When Richie answered the phone the first words I said were, "We did it, Tommy, Luzzi, and I went to Trenton yesterday to the boxing commission office. After a few touch and go moments, we were able to obtain the boxing license."

Richie replied, "Honestly Doc, I didn't believe that you would ever get the license."

I came back at Rich, "DESTINY."

Rich then said that he also had good news, he said, "The board of education for the high school that I was principal for all those years has booked you for a speaking engagement that is scheduled for this Friday morning."

I was elated after hearing the news that Rich brought forth. I then expressed to Rich that I thought he was doing a great job and how much I appreciated his dedication and effort toward the mission.

I then told Rich that I wanted him to attend my speaking engagement at the old high school that he ran. I could tell from his body language that he was happy to hear that.

After saying that, I let Rich know that I would like him to attend every speaking engagement that I have from now on. I told him that I wanted him to be the orchestra conductor, making sure that from the time we arrive to when we leave that everything would run perfectly.

Rich agreed by saying, "Doc, you are right, it's very important that everything we do is done in a most efficient and professional manner.

We left off by me telling Rich to pick me up Friday, an hour and a half before I was scheduled to speak.

The next morning, I was sitting, having a cup of coffee with Tommy and Luzzi in the lounge of the racquetball club.

I guess you could say that the three of us were still gloating over our achievement yesterday for obtaining the boxing license.

Tommy then said, "Ok Doc, now that we have the license, what is our next step?"

Before I could answer, Luzzi said, "I know, Doc has to get into shape to pass the physical and be ready for his fight."

Luzzi then said, "Doc, you have to immediately start running, I know that for a fact. Every fighter has to run miles every day to build up their endurance before a fight."

After Luzzi spoke, I started to laugh before I said, "I can't run, I have a really bad knee. It comes out of its socket every so often. I should have gotten surgery again some time ago."

Luzzi then busted out laughing as he said, "Are you kidding me, you can't run, how the hell are you going to be a fighter?"

"Without running before a fight, you won't be able to last more than a round or two, I'm sure you know this."

Tommy then said, "Doc, please forget this crazy shit, you can't even run, how the hell are you going to fight? You won't even be able to last a round or two."

I then said, "Relax fellas, I have the answer, I'll just have to stop my opponent before I run out of gas."

Tommy then said, "Oh my God, we're the gang that can't shoot straight." Luzzi then said, "It's like going to fight in Vietnam with a BB gun." I then replied, "DESTINY" my good fellas, "DESTINY."

Yeah, yeah, yeah, was Tommy's remark, before he asked the question, "What's the agenda today?"

I replied, "I'm going to Bufano's Boxing Gym in Jersey City to do some sparring. I'm going to also do some work on the heavy and speed bag."

I then told the guys that they didn't have to come. Tommy then said, "Are you telling me that you're going to be going into the ring to do some boxing?"

I replied, "That's what sparring means Tom."

Tommy then said, "Are you kidding me, I won't miss this opportunity for anything!" He then asked the question again, "Doc, are you telling me that today you're going to go into the ring with a professional fighter?"

I replied, most likely, yes. Only if there are not many fighters at the gym during the time that we arrive, I might not spar.

Luzzi then said, "Bufano's Gym, are you talking about that old broken-down building that you took me to fifty years ago to see Sonny Liston train before he fought Chuck Wepner?"

I replied, "You got it right, the grandkids now run the gym."

John then said, "I remember a section of the floor where I felt like I was going to fall right through to the first floor." We all started laughing after Luzzi's remark.

I then said, ok, it's settled, you guys are coming with me later to the gym, come pick me up at 3 o'clock. I have to go to my nephew's basement where I still have many of my belongings since I went to prison.

I have to get my boxing shoes, speed bag, and boxing gloves that Chuck Wepner gave me as a gift. They were the training gloves that he used before his fight with Mohammad Ali.

I then told the guys, "Please try and look like you're trainers, don't come all dressed up in your designer outfits, come with sweatshirts and jeans or a jogging outfit."

Three o'clock on the button the limo pulls up to Brian's home. When I entered the vehicle there sat Tommy and Johnny wearing their $500 jogging outfits and their $400 designer sneakers.

After seeing how they were dressed, I didn't make a comment, why bother. I then said to myself, *I guess it's better than if they had worn one of their $4,000 suits.*

As we were getting close to the gym, I told the limo driver, "The gym is two blocks down on the left-hand side."

Of course, Luzzi chimed in with his sarcastic humor when he said, "I can see the neighborhood hasn't changed in the past fifty years." How could Tommy and I not laugh at that remark?

When we arrived at the dilapidated building that was located on the corner, one could not help but notice how badly in need the old wooden structure was, thirsty for a few coats of paint.

We parked the limo directly in front of the gym not realizing the commotion that would eventually cause.

As we entered the dark gloomy hallway and started to climb the many steps it would take to get to the second floor where the gym was located, as we took each step the stairs began to squeak the same way they did fifty years ago.

Being in that dark hallway and walking up those squeaky steps gave you the impression that you are walking into a haunted house rather than into a boxing gym.

When we entered the gym, we heard the loud repetitive popping sound of the speed bags banging back and forth. There were also the thunderous sounds of fists blasting against the leather bags. We also heard the bouncing sound of fighters jumping up and down as they were skipping rope.

The way that our sense of hearing immediately heard the sounds of a boxing gym, that was the same way our sense of smell was affected when we walked into a cloud of body odor.

After telling Tommy and Luzzi to be seated in the area where the spectators sit during their training and sparring, I then went to the Bufano grandson and introduced myself, he then told me that his name was Dom, the same as his grandfather.

I told Dom, "I used to come and train here fifty years ago when your grandfather ran the joint." After paying him dues for a year ahead of time plus a very big tip, I asked Dom if he could make arrangements to have one of the pro fighters' spar a round or two with me after I warm up.

Dom couldn't react any faster when he said, "Don't worry I will take care of anything you need." I knew he meant what he said because nobody pays their dues a year in advance, not to even mention the size of the tip that I gave him.

ᑲᔥᕕᏇChapter Four᙭᙭

I left the house already dressed and prepared for my workout. I had my jockstrap on with my boxing shorts along with my sweat outfit. All I had to do was slip into my boxing shoes; I came there already dressed because I had no intention after my workout to shower there.

The first thing I decided to do for warming up was to skip rope. Not only is it good for warming up but it also helps with your coordination, reflexes and timing.

As I began to skip rope my timing was off, and I was finding it difficult to skip the rope with the proper rhythm. After being persistent, I was starting to get the hang of it.

As I glanced over to Tommy and Luzzi they had a look of disappointment on their face. I then decided to go over to the heavy bag. After putting on the bag gloves, I began to hit the heavy bag.

Then, out of the corner of one eye, I saw all the fighters stopping whatever they were doing standing there with their mouths wide open. Their eyes could not believe what they were seeing as they watched me throw punches at a lightning speed.

When they saw the force of the punches as my fist hit into that bag that echoed throughout the gym, they were in total amazement.

They continued to watch and saw how I was able to throw left hooks and right crosses with such power and precision. Left jabs were being thrown, and when hitting the leather bag, it sounded like the rat-a-tat-tat of machine gunfire. The straight right punch when contact was made with the heavy bag sounded like a shotgun blast.

The boxers couldn't believe this could come from a man of my age. As all this is happening, with the fighters watching, at the other end of the gym there are people coming in from the street.

The reason people were attracted to the gym was because the limo was parked directly in front of the gym. A limousine parked in that neighborhood brought curiosity from the people in that area wondering who might be in the gym.

Of course, as most people were entering the gym, they were expecting to see one of the world boxing champions having a workout.

During this time, Dom came up to me and asked if I was ready to spar a round or two. When I told him yes, he introduced me to a young and upcoming fighter named Jorge.

Jorge had four professional fights so far with a 3 and 1 record. He appeared to be six foot two inches tall, approximately 220 pounds.

At this time both Dom and Jorge had no idea that I was considering becoming a fighter again. They just assumed that I was being adventurous at my old age wanting to spar with a pro.

Dom was the one who assisted me by putting the sparring headgear on me along with the boxing cup to protect my coconuts. After he rubbed some Vaseline on my face, he said, "Ok fellas box."

As I looked over to Tommy and Luzzi, I could see from the expression on their face how excited they now were, nothing like the look on their face when I started to skip rope.

It appeared like they were still gloating from when I was hitting the heavy bag.

As Jorge and I were sparring, it was so obvious to see that Dom instructed Jorge to go easy on me. Nevertheless, I felt comfortable out there. My footwork was good, and I was throwing sharp punches and combinations.

After the three minutes ended the round, I decided to go one more being that Jorge was going easy on me.

When the sparring was completed, I hugged Jorge and thanked him for the workout. One thing about the sport of boxing and that is most fighters have great respect for one another.

After walking over to Dom to thank him, I then called to Tom and John to come over so I could introduce them to Dom. I then told Tom that I'm going to be coming in most days for a workout to get into shape, and these guys are going to accompany me.

I was hoping that as we come in you could teach the guys how to tape hands and some of the other formalities of being a trainer. Dom's response was, "Doc, I already told you, anything you need, I will take care of you."

As we exited the building, there were a number of curious people hanging out around the limo waiting and hoping to see some big celebrity. As we were getting ready to enter the limo, there was this kid that looked to be about fifteen, he came up to me and said, "Who are you?" I answered his question by saying, "I'm the next heavyweight champion of the world."

He looked at me with a puzzled look as he said, "No way!"

As we headed toward home Tommy and John were acting like two kids about to open their presents on Christmas morning.

They were so excited and showing optimism for the first time after seeing me in the gym. It was then that I had to bust their bubble by saying, "listen fellas, punching a heavy bag is no big deal, you must always remember that heavy bags don't punch back."

Don't get me wrong, I was happy that I was able to show hand speed and power in my delivery after all these years.

Now, as for the sparring, Jorge treated me in the ring for exactly who I am, a seventy-two-year-old man.

"Again, don't get me wrong fellas, I was pleased with my footwork and the way I moved, but that was no test for what is about to come."

After saying what I said to the guys, I then started to truly analyze in my mind the hard facts of reality. I then said to myself, *"My only chance in a million will be if the supernatural strength enters my body during each of my fights."*

As the guys were dropping me off at my son's house, I told them that I had a speaking engagement at 10:00 a.m. tomorrow. I mentioned that Rich made the arrangements; I will be speaking in front of the high school that Rich served as the principal for many years.

When I suggested Tom and John pick me up at three o'clock tomorrow to go to the gym, Tommy eagerly responded, "Why can't we come to hear you speak?" Hearing those words was a surprise to me. If I had to guess, I would say that Tommy is starting to become enthusiastic about what we're trying to do ever since we went to the gym.

Luzzi then expressed that he also had an interest in hearing me speak. He said to me, "I've been curious to know what the hell you speak about?" He then added, "Let's face it, you're no Einstein."

Tommy and I both, laughed after hearing that comment. I then said, "Ok, it's settled, you guys are going to be coming with Rich and me to the high school. Rich is coming to pick me up at 8:30 a.m., so why don't you guys meet us at my son's house at 8:30 tomorrow morning?"

Tommy then said, "We'll all go over to the high school in the limo, perhaps if the school staff sees our entourage exiting the limo they might be impressed." That brought a laugh to everyone.

The next day Richie was the first to arrive, so I told him that Tommy and Luzzi were going to be coming with us. I told him that we will all ride over to the school in the limo.

When Tom and John showed up, I let them know that they could help Richie give out my books and pamphlets on "Doc's Five Ingredients to Success in Life."

As we were riding over to the school, Tommy and Luzzi were telling Richie about our experience at the gym the day before. When Tommy kept going on and on, Luzzi said, maybe we should be quiet so that Doc can concentrate on what he's going to speak about.

I responded to Luzzi's comment with a laugh at first before I said, just like my writing, whatever insight is given to me at the moment is the subject matter that I speak about. Truth be told, I'm only capable of speaking when I'm inspired to do so.

When we arrived at the high school we were greeted by the entire administrative staff. Actually, they were all excited seeing Richie since they were all employed at the school when Rich was principal.

It was the present-day principal who introduced me to the student body. When I began to speak, the first thing I said was, "Oh my, I'm having a brain freeze. I'm not quite sure the topic and message that I had intended to bring forth this morning."

After making that comment, you had to see the expression on Rich, Tom, and John's face. They looked as white as a ghost and you could see that they had fear in their eyes not knowing what was going to come next.

I then said to the student body, "I hope you don't get angry at me, at least I got you out of the classroom." That comment brought laughter from the audience.

I then said, "When I was in prison, yes, I was in prison; I became close with the prison Rabbi. He had heard about the mentoring I was doing with the inmates. He had also read all my books.

After getting to know him, he would come and spend countless hours standing at the gate of my cell talking with me.

Most of our time would be philosophizing about life. I remember one time he came up to me after he just completed reading my last book, "The Psycho Club."

The Rabbi said to me, "Of course I'm aware that you only write to bring forth a message." He then said, "I believe your number one message that you were trying to convey to the reader in "The Psycho Club" was, as long as your alive, there is always hope. As long as you have air in your lungs and your heart is still pumping blood through your body, you are capable of changing things in your life."

You must also remember that being alive, you also have the opportunity of righting wrong.

Once life leaves your body that is the last final chapter of your life. That's the end of your book, the final chapter of your life is over and there could be no more.

The Rabbi then said, "Your message to always hold on to life reminds me of these three Rabbis that were talking about life and death when the question came up: 'When you're in your casket, and friends and congregants are mourning over you, what would you like them to say?"

The first Rabbi said: "I would like them to say I was a wonderful husband, a fine spiritual leader and a great family man."

The second Rabbi commented: "I would like them to say I was a wonderful teacher and servant of God who made a huge difference in people's lives."

The third Rabbi thought for a moment and remarked: "I'd like them to say, "Look, he's moving!""

That comment brought much laughter from the student body. At that moment I looked over to the guys and I could notice a sigh of relief on their faces.

The first subject that I began to speak on was imagination. I let the student body realize that this is a very special gift given to all of us and few people are aware of this special gift.

I let the audience know that as special as a gift that it is to everyone, your imagination is extremely most important to a young person.

It's so important that you have the awareness that anything you're capable of imagining is obtainable as long as what you're imagining feels natural to you.

I then started to get a little emotional when I said in a deep stern voice, "Your imagination is yours and only yours, you should never allow anyone to tamper with it."

It's important that we are aware that anything that mankind has accomplished on planet earth had to be first imagined before it was created.

By this time, I became in the moment, I was in the zone from "Beyond the Beyond."

As I continued on bringing forth many important messages of self-worth, I was doing it with such inspiration that everyone including, Tom, John, and Rich could not believe how motivated and inspired the crowd had become.

I would have to say by the time I completed speaking, not only was the student body mesmerized, but also the faculty.

During the time that the guys were handing out my pamphlets and a copy of the Godfather of Souls to each student, I was in the principal's office being thanked by the entire administrative staff for my talk to the students.

Each one assured me that they were looking forward to reading all of my books. The principal left off by saying to me that there is an open invitation to speak to his students.

As we were getting into the limo it was clear to see that after hearing me speak it had an effect on the guys. They were showing incredible enthusiasm and were motivated like I haven't seen before.

My observation was confirmed when I heard Luzzi say, "You had the crowd so motivated that you had me wanting to get into the ring." Tommy excitedly said, "you had the entire crowd all pumped up, even the faculty."

Rich had a big smile on his face because he knew that my performance made him look good.

When we arrived in Rutherford, I suggested that we all go to the Lyndhurst Diner for lunch. I then said after that, Rich could go home, and we'll go early to Bufano's Gym for my workout.

Rich sounded like a little boy that was being punished, when he said, "Why can't I come with you guys to the gym?"

After Tommy had Richie's ear about our visit to the gym yesterday, I'm not surprised at all that Richie wanted to come to the gym.

Of course you can come to the gym with us, is how I answered Rich. I then said, "I thought you might have other things to do." Rich's response was, "I'm retired, I'm into this thing with you guys all the way."

When the waitress came to take our order, the pain started to enter my body. Luzzi ordered a fresh turkey club sandwich with American cheese, bacon, with lettuce and tomato. Tommy had a lean roast beef club sandwich; the lean beef was piled so high. It was accompanied by ripe slices of tomatoes and horseradish sauce.

Rich had this humongous charred medium-rare burger with melted cheddar cheese, bacon, and lettuce and tomato. All three of the guys had side orders of these large plump potato wedges with brown gravy on the side.

After seeing all that, it was quite difficult to even look at my cottage cheese and fruit platter.

After lunch we made a quick stop at my son Brian's house so I could pick up my workout bag, and then we were off to the gym.

When we arrived at the gym, we were all interested in seeing Richie's reaction to what he was seeing. It all started when Rich observed the dilapidated building that housed the gym.

When we all entered the dark gloomy hallway and began to climb those squeaky steps, Rich made his first comment when he turned to me and said, "Is this the gym that John L. Sullivan trained at?" We all started to laugh from that comment.

When we entered the gym and Rich observed all the activity that was going on, his body language showed that he was excited about being there. I then told the guys to go sit in the spectator area while I go speak to Dom.

I told Tom and John "Before I start my workout, I have to discuss a very important matter with Dom; I will fill you guys in later on what I'm doing."

When I looked for Dom, he was nowhere on the workout floor, so I went to his office. After knocking on the door, I shouted out, "It's Doc." I entered after Dom invited me in.

Dom then asked how he could help me. My response was, "I'm happy that you're sitting down." I then told Dom that I would like him to get me a professional fight; of course he started to laugh.

Along with Tom and John, I would like you to represent me as manager-trainer. Dom, with a puzzled look on his face said, "You're not kidding, are you?" He then said no boxing promoter would ever give a seventy-two-year-old man a fight on his card.

I responded to Dom's opinion by saying, "If you listen to my advice, I promise you that you will get the fight for me."

Dom came back at me, "Doc, please listen to me, I instructed Jorge to be very fragile with you during your sparring session yesterday."

I started to laugh, Dom, that's not why I'm asking you to get me a fight; of course I know that you instructed Jorge to go easy on me. You just have to trust me why I want to go back into the ring and that I know what I'm doing.

Dom still had a look of skepticism on his face when I said, "If you listen to me, you will sell the promoter to give you the fight."

I then prepared Dom by informing him that when you come to the promoter representing a seventy-two- year old boxer, his first response will be laughter, until you enlighten him on how he could earn extra money. That will get his attention real fast.

You first have to sell the promoter that this old man has a great following and will fill all the empty seats. Your second selling point has to be the unique way that an old man is going into the ring, risking his life, just to try and do the impossible.

The third point is that despite his age of seventy-two, he has exceptional strength and is exceptionally tough.

Dom, you also have to remind the promoter that the contract will protect him against any harm to your fighter. I then told Dom to tell the promoter to get a journeyman, a fighter that's getting ready to retire.

Resorts Casino in Atlantic City was putting on boxing shows every Tuesday night, some were even televised. I suggested to Dom that he go see the promoter who runs the boxing shows for Resorts.

I let Dom know that I wanted him to take both Tom and John along with him to the meeting.

After giving all that advice to Dom, I then hinted to him that if he was successful in fulfilling my request, it would be well worth his effort.

I then squinted, looking directly into Dom's eyes and said, "Truth be told, if you do what I say, I assure you that we will get the fight, it's DESTINY."

After saying what I said, Dom got up from behind his desk, and with a tone of confidence in his voice, he said, "Ok Doc, let me start to get you into shape.

When we entered the main area of the gym, Dom called for Tommy and Luzzi who were sitting with Richie in the spectator area.

Once Tom and Luz walked over, Dom said to them, "ok fellas, you have to watch and learn how to tape up hands.

After my hands were taped, the guys went back to sit with Richie as I started to skip rope. Once I completed skipping rope, I went to the speed bag and then followed up by pounding the heavy bag.

I could tell that Rich was enjoying seeing me showoff my hand speed as I made that speed bag sing. His eyes were wide open as he watched my fist crush into the heavy bag.

After completing my bag work, I went into the ring to do a few rounds of shadow boxing before I finished off my work out by doing calisthenics such as pushups and sit-ups.

By the time I finished my workout, Dom came up to me and said, "I called the promoter from Resorts Casino in Atlantic City. I have an appointment to meet with him tomorrow morning at 10:00 o'clock."

Hearing that news brought great joy and excitement to me. Thinking that it was a two-hour ride to Atlantic City, I told Dom that Tom and John would pick him up in the limo at the gym at 7:00 a.m. tomorrow morning.

After leaving the gym as we were headed toward home, I started to fill the guys in on what's going on. I asked Tom and John if they would be able to pick up Dom at the gym tomorrow morning at 7:00 a.m. sharp.

I explained the reason was because Dom had a 10:00 a.m. appointment with the boxing promoter for Resorts Casino in A.C. I then explained to them that being that they were very successful salesmen in their own business; I wanted them to help Dom sell the promoter in giving me a fight.

Tom and John simultaneously responded by eagerly saying, "We'll be there."

It was only after getting Tom and John's commitment that I realized that I had already made the arrangements for them to meet Dom tomorrow to go to Atlantic City.

After having that thought, I answered myself by saying, *"I just knew that they would be there for me."*

Richie then said, "So, it's possible you could be in the ring fighting as early as two weeks?" Luzzi showed concern over that statement when he said, "You will never be in shape for a fight in that short of time."

"No, no, no," is how I responded to Luzzi's statement. I then said to the guys, "Truth be told, at my age I could never get into shape to fight in the ring no matter how long I train."

Fellas, don't worry about me being in shape; you guys just go ahead and get me the fight, hopefully as soon as possible. I let the guys know that as long as I'm able to pass the physical the day of the fight, I'm good to go.

I then reminded the guys that I have no time to waste with the game plan that I'm on. All I need to rely on is DESTINY!

As the guys were dropping me off at my son's house, I made arrangements with Richie to pick me up at 2:30 tomorrow afternoon so he could take me to the gym for my workout. I then told Tom and John that when they return from A.C., we will all meet at the gym at 4:00 o'clock.

Right before I exited the limo, I challenged Tom and John by saying, "Let's see how really good you guys are as salesmen."

ᏩᏕᎡᏃChapter FiveᏁᏛᎡᏒ

When the next day arrived, I was anxious to get to the gym for my workout. I have no doubt it was because of the anticipation that I was experiencing not knowing how Dom and the guys made out with the boxing promoter.

I could tell that Richie was feeling the same as me even though he didn't talk about it.

Would you believe the timing was perfect? At the very moment that I finished doing my final push-up that completed my workout, Dom, Tom, and John came walking into the gym from Atlantic City.

The first words out of Dom's mouth were, "Let's all go into my office."

As we were all walking into Dom's office it was easy for me to read from all their body language that they had good news. As soon as we all sat down, Dom said, "You got your fight." He then said, "You also had another wish granted, the fight is next week."

That's when Tommy jumped in and said, "We got lucky, the promoter told us that an up and coming heavyweight on the undercard had to cancel. He was going to be fighting a thirty-eight-year-old journeyman, who now is going to be your opponent."

Dom then said the promoter was skeptical at first, but after hearing Tommy and John speak along with me, we were able to flip him. Dom then said, "It was a team effort."

I then turned to Tommy and Luzzi and said, "I guess you guys are pretty good salesmen." That remark had gotten Luzzi all stirred up and he turned to me and said, "Doc, I knew we had the promoter when I told him that he was going to wind up making more money from the uniqueness of having an old man on the card."

Tommy then responded by saying, "I guess it also didn't hurt the situation that I invited the promoter to come eat with us at Resort's elegant steakhouse."

That's when Dom said to me, "Doc, I ate the best steak I ever had in my life, it was worth the $100 dollar price tag on it."

Tommy responded by saying, "Of course we didn't have to pay for anything, we received everything on comp."

Luzzi's braggadocio showed when he said, "Not only did we not pay for lunch at the steakhouse, Tommy also won $3,000 dollars and I won $11,000 playing blackjack."

When I became privy to that information, I responded by saying, "That's great news; you guys could now donate half of your winnings to purchase my books so that we can send them to prisons."

Tommy kiddingly said to Luzzi, "Oh shit, you have a motor mouth!" I then turned to Tommy and said, "If you weren't going to Atlantic City for the cause, you would have not been going to Atlantic City."

Luzzi started to laugh as he said, "Yeah, that's right, if we weren't going to A.C. for Doc, we would have not been going there anyway." We all started to laugh at that comment.

We all then said good-bye to Dom before I told him that we would all see him tomorrow for my workout.

Dom then turned to Tommy and said, "I'm going to dream about that steak that we had for lunch." Tommy responded to Dom as we were walking out of the gym by saying, "Dom, next week after Doc gets his ass beaten, as long as he doesn't swallow his dentures, we will all go to the steakhouse after the fight for a late dinner."

As we were in the limo driving back home, I told Rich that since he is the publicist, it was his job to go on the computer and lookup Everlast Boxing Equipment; they're located in New York City.

"Rich, I need you to get three red silk trainer jackets, two larges for Dom and Luzzi, and one extra-large for Tommy. They all have to say Grandpa Doc in white lettering on the back of each jacket."

I then told Richie, "I need an extra-large white silk robe with red lettering saying Grandpa Doc on the back of the robe." I also requested white silk extra-large boxing trunks with a red stripe on each side.

During the next six days leading up to fight night, we were all busy trying to prepare for the event. Dom was schooling Tommy and Luzzi on what their assignments will be the night of the fight.

Dom instructed Tommy that his responsibility will be to bring the ice water bucket up into the corner of the ring in between rounds. Dom told him to make sure that there is a square piece of metal with a handle in the bucket.

Dom explained to Tom that the metal plate would be applied by him to any area of Doc's face that would show swelling. He also instructed Tom to make sure he had a small jar of Vaseline in one of his jacket pockets.

Dom then told Luzzi that he will be responsible for bringing the stool up into the corner for Doc to sit on in between rounds. He also instructed John to have ammonia capsules in his one jacket pocket and a squirt water bottle in the other pocket.

Dom then told both Tommy and Luzzi that once the bell rings to end the round, he will immediately climb the steps and jump into the ring to administer to Doc. Dom said, "Simultaneously, I need you two to climb the steps and then lean over between the ropes, one on each side of Doc so that you can assist me."

Dom then told Luzzi that after he brings the stool up into the corner of the ring; he's then responsible for taking the mouthpiece out of Doc's mouth during the one-minute rest.

Of course, Luzzi had to offer a sarcastic remark when he said, "Dom, I'm assuming you mean to take the entire package out of Doc's mouth, teeth included," everyone started laughing.

It seemed like within a flash I was waking up and it was the day of the fight. We had all left Dom, Tommy, Luzzi, Richie, and me the day before the fight to go to Atlantic City.

We were all given separate rooms from the strength of the power ratings from Tommy and Luzzi's casino play.

That all worked out perfectly because I was keeping my fight a secret from my son and daughter-in-law. I just told them that I was going away for a few days with my friends to Atlantic City.

On the morning of the fight, we all went to a restaurant inside Resorts for breakfast. I could sense that all the guys were more nervous and concerned about the weigh-in and physical that was scheduled for 12:00 o'clock noon.

When it was time for the physical and weigh-in, I wasn't nervous at all. I was confident that I was going to pass the physical.

The way things turned out; I passed the physical with flying colors. Blood pressure was perfect; heart rate was excellent along with all the other tests.

Getting on the scale found me overweight at 254 pounds, but it was better than the 280 pounds that I weighed before I started training.

It's the night of the fight; Dom is taping my hands, as Tommy and Luzzi are on both sides of him trying to assist by holding the scissors, gauze and tape.

After they put the boxing gloves on me, it was only minutes away from me leaving the dressing room to make the lonely walk to the ring.

As I started to walk down the aisle to the ring, I was shocked to notice that there was not one empty seat.

Normally, when you're the first fight scheduled on the card, only half the crowd has arrived by then to watch the first fight.

It then came to me; the promoter took Luzzi's advice and promoted the uniqueness of having a seventy-two-year-old man on the undercard.

As I am starting to climb into the ring, I noticed the extra lighting, and I remember that the fight was being shown live on TV. That is when I realized that thousands upon thousands of people were watching me in their homes at that very moment.

My childhood dreams were starting to become a reality. I then started to reminisce back to over fifty years ago when I was standing in the ring in front of the TV cameras winning the New Jersey State boxing championship.

As I'm warming up moments before the start of the fight, I take notice how professional and good Dom and the guys looked in those beautiful new cherry red satin boxing jackets with the white lettering saying, "Grandpa Doc."

When Dom started to take my shiny white satin robe off me, *I then began to say to myself, once the bell rings I must concentrate on having a thought that is going to stir-up my emotions so that I can obtain this supernatural strength. I did realize that would be my only chance of winning the fight.*

Before the bell rang to start the fight, I did say a short prayer that this newfound unexplainable strength that is given to me does not seriously hurt my opponent.

When the bell rang, I came out dancing on my toes like I used to when I was young, despite my size I always had great footwork.

As I looked at my opponent, he appeared to be much bigger standing in front of me in the ring, rather than when we sat alongside each other at the weigh-in.

He looked to be in excellent shape standing tall at six-one and weighing 230 even though he started out slow. I believe he started out slow because he was having compassion seeing an old man in front of him.

Nevertheless, he caught me with a left hook to my solar plexus. The pain was so great that I want to go down to one knee just to catch my breath, but I chose not to. I'm gasping for air, trying so hard not to show on my face the pain I'm enduring.

I felt he was purposely going through the motions the first round because of my age. As he continued to be non-aggressive the first round, the fans started to boo him.

They were all yelling and screaming, "You bum, you can't even knock out an old man."

I could now see that my opponent was becoming embarrassed and very angry when the bell rang to end the first round.

As I started to walk toward the corner, I saw Dom jumping into the ring and Tommy on the top step leaning his upper body through the ropes. When I reached the corner, there was no stool to sit on. When Dom noticed that he started yelling, "Where is the damned stool?"

At that moment the fans that were sitting close to my corner started yelling to Luzzi, "Bring them the stool."

The reason Luzzi wasn't paying attention was because he was sitting on the stool being distracted by a beautiful model wearing a skimpy bikini with high heels. She was parading around the ring holding this large cardboard sign saying, "Round Two."

When the crowd was finally able to get Luzzi's attention to bring Dom the stool, Luzzi started to turn around to look for the stool, that's when the crowd nearest to the corner yelled out to Luzzi, "you're sitting on it," as they continued to hysterically laugh.

By the time Luzzi brought the stool up to the corner there were only a few seconds remaining before the bell rang for round two.

Unlike the first round where my opponent came out slow, this round he came out with blood in his eyes. It was obvious that the crowd embarrassed my opponent and made him really furious.

My first thought was to try to dance and stay away from him while I try to stir-up my emotions so I can receive the super strength, the problem was as hard as I was trying, nothing was happening.

At that moment my opponent came recklessly at me in such a violent way with his right arm cocked ready to take my head off. I was too tired to run and dance anymore, so I went toward him throwing a straight right hand that landed right on his jaw, he went crashing to the canvas, the way the twin towers went crashing to the ground.

He laid there long after the count of ten. Even though the superpower never entered my body during the fight, even in my old age I always knew that I still had a great amount of my punching power from years gone by.

What had concerned me was that I was unable to share my dilemma with anyone as to why I hadn't received the special power that has been entering my body each time I become emotional.

I was really puzzled about that and knew that despite winning this fight, I could never continue on without knowing if I was going to receive this special power ever again.

Because of all the excitement after the fight, I decided to put that last thought on the back burner for the moment.

Ten minutes after the knockout and the fight ending, the crowd was still really buzzing and full of electricity. Dom, Tom, John, and Rich were flying as high as a kite, and the TV announcers were still talking about my fight throughout the entire boxing card and broadcast.

After I showered and got dressed, I told the guys that we could watch the remaining fights at the steakhouse. I informed the guys that the steakhouse has large screen TVs and they're broadcasting tonight's fight card.

I can't even begin to tell you how happy that suggestion meant to Dom, but I must say, even Richie was also showing a real lot of excitement from my suggestion.

The next morning, we all got up early despite being up till the wee hours of the morning throwing the dice. We were going to one of the many restaurants in the hotel for breakfast.

I decided to treat myself after being on a stringent diet the past thirty days. So, I ordered steak and eggs with crispy home fries, a large stack of buttermilk pancakes with apple compote and whipped butter. I then had a large fruit cup, not as a main course, but as a side. WOW! I sure did enjoy that!

After breakfast, we all made a pact to stay clear of the casino. We headed directly to our rooms to get packed and then we were on our way back home.

While riding in the limo, I instructed Dom to get me another fight within the next month. I told him that it's most important that he do this right away, I have no time to waste.

Dom came back at me by saying, "That time frame is much too soon, you have to recuperate."

I then responded, "Recuperate from what, I don't have a scratch on me!"

I then grabbed Dom's hand and said, "Please believe me, I know my destiny, get me a fight as soon as possible."

I then turned to Richie and said, "I now need you to concentrate on getting me new speaking engagements, regardless of how small they might be." I then said, "Rich, I will find the time in between my training and fighting to do my speaking, that's most important."

Turning to Tom and John, I said, "I need you guys to apply to set up a nonprofit corporation, you shall name it, "Beyond the Beyond."

I want you two to be the chief officers, Tommy being the oldest, I want you to be president and make Luzzi vice-president. Richie began to clear his throat in a way that got my attention, I then said, "In fact, make Richie the Secretary of the corporation."

"You guys are going to be perfect candidates for these positions; you all have had impeccable, honest and clean records your entire lives."

I then told the guys that any money that will be earned through my fighting or my speaking engagements will be donated to Beyond the Beyond.

"That will allow us to purchase my books and distribute them throughout the prison system in the country. Of course, all profits from my books will also be donated to the corporation."

I continued by saying "The only money that will be taken out of the corporation will be for our business expenses and Dom's salary while I continue to fight."

That last statement had made Dom irate, as he turned to me with a nasty look and in an angry tone of voice said, "You expect me to take a salary when all of you are donating your time for the cause? " I don't want no salary."

Dom then said, "It probably won't matter anyway, the odds are great that your boxing career will be ended next fight."

I laughed at Dom's remark, but deep down inside of me I was reminded that I had to find a way to assure myself that when I entered the ring; I would receive this super unexplainable strength.

I knew that I had to stir-up my emotions in a way that I could assure myself that this unexplainable strength will enter my body at the right time.

I know that I'm not delusional, I know that the only chance that I have of winning another fight is to receive this mystery strength.

That thought was starting to become trying on my mind and I was getting depressed. So, to forget that thought, I started to ask the guys if they won or lost when we all went to gamble after dinner last night.

Tommy was the first to answer, "I broke even." Richie and Dom followed by saying the same thing. Luzzi then started to laugh as he said, "I broke even too."

I started to bust out laughing as I accused them all of being lying bastards. I'm sure they were in fear that I would have taken half of their winnings.

After accusing them of lying, I said to them, "I wish I had the lie detector robot that I talked about in one of my books." The way that they all laughed, I believe that they remembered the story. Nevertheless, Tommy said, "Doc, tell it again."

I responded to Tommy's request by saying, "I'll try my best to remember the story."

One night a father brought home a lie detector robot to dinner. Each time someone would tell a lie the robot would slap the person. So, while eating the father asked the son, "So where were you last night?"

The son replied, "I was with my friend at the library."

The robot slapped the son. So, the son then said, "Ok, I was at my friend's house studying." The robot slapped the son again.

The son then said, "Ok, I was at my friend's house watching porn."

The father replied, "How could you have done something as disgusting as that?" When I was your age, we would never do anything like that. The robot turned and slapped the father. The mother started to laugh as she replied, "He sure is your son," the robot turned and slapped the mother.

When we arrived up North, Dom was the first to be dropped off. When I told him that I'll see him at the gym tomorrow for my workout he responded by saying, "Take a few days off."

I came back at Dom by saying, "I can't afford to take off, time is of the essence, just concentrate on getting me another fight as soon as possible."

Dom shook his head and said, "I'll see you guys tomorrow."

I was the next to be dropped off; I said good-bye to the guys and told them that I'd see them at 3:00 o'clock tomorrow.

When I entered the house, my son, Brian was waiting for me like a father would wait for a son who has broken curfew. He then nonchalantly said to me, "Did you have a good time in A.C.?"

I responded by saying, "Yes, we ate at the steakhouse and none of us lost any money."

My son came back at me by saying, "And you didn't get knocked out, you forgot to tell me that, Grandpa Doc."

I started to laugh as I said, "What are you talking about?"

Brian responded, "Dad, Michael Clark saw you on TV fighting in the ring at Resorts Casino, or are you telling me that there is another old man that calls himself Grandpa Doc and coincidentally looks just like you?"

"Michael tried calling me during the fight, but my cell phone was off because I was scouting new players for my team."

Brian then said, "Dad, are you losing your mind? Are you crazy? A man of your age could easily get killed in the ring."

I responded to my son's concern by saying, "Son, you're just going to have to trust me that I know what I'm doing, I don't want you to worry."

I then told Brian not to tell his brothers and sister at this time about my fighting. He sounded quite annoyed when he said, "I'm not going to tell anyone, you better know what you're doing because we all love you."

Brian then said, "Mommy sent you a letter." He was referring to his mother, the mother of my four children. Louise has a house in Florida, right next door to my daughter, Gina's home.

When I was in prison for the last seven years, Louise always wrote me to keep me informed on how my four children were doing. She did the same with my eleven grandchildren. Even though I was absent from my family, she helped to keep me part of their lives, and for that I will always love her and be grateful to her.

From the very first time that I became a father up until the present time, I have given thanks for being blessed to have her as the mother of my children.

When I opened the letter from Louise, I was about to receive the greatest compliment that I could ever imagine being bestowed on me. I make this evaluation from the past record of the mother that Louise has been to my children.

Despite the many downfalls that occurred throughout my life, that had an effect on me being a father, I have always loved my children unconditionally.

Through the years I have tried to slowly become more and more part of their lives to show my love for them.

Perhaps that might have had something to do with the letter she wrote to me saying the words: "there would be no other man that I would have wanted to be the father of my children than you."

Reading those words immediately brought tears to my eyes, I became extremely emotional in a way that words would be hard to explain.

What I do know is that if I won the Heisman Trophy, Heavyweight Championship, wrote the record-breaking best-selling book, or won the multi-million-dollar lottery would have not given me the euphoria that I experienced from those words.

Little did I know at that time how great an impact those words were going to have on my destiny.

The next week I put much time into my training because I had a strong premonition that Dom was going to arrange a fight for me in the very near future.

Even though my efforts at the time were to physically condition my body, my mind and concentration were on Tommy and Luzzi's efforts to create the non-profit corporation.

Richie's success in setting up speaking engagements for me was also most important because this is where my passion lies. This is also where I will be completing my final purpose in life.

I no longer have the passion for the sport of boxing like I once did. I no longer hunger to be the ultimate warrior-like in the early years of my youth. I no longer have the determination to make the physical effort and sacrifice it takes to be the best.

I no longer have any of the important qualities that are needed to achieve such an incredible feat as the one I pursue. All I have is my belief in my insight in knowing my destiny.

ᴄ◡◠Chapter Six◠◡ᴐ

After a week back in the gym my premonition became a reality when Dom came up to me with the news that the promoter from Resorts Casino gave him a call, "He wants to put you back on his boxing card scheduled for three weeks."

Dom went on to say, "I could see from the promoter's mo-jo that he was quite pleased with your performance and the way things turned out during your first fight."

Dom explained that the opponent would be a twenty-five-year-old, six-foot, 200-pound fighter with a 2 and 0 pro-record. He did warn me that this guy had an extensive successful amateur career before he turned pro.

I eagerly responded without hesitation from the information that Dom provided to me by saying, "Take the fight, I have no time to waste."

The same day that I was given the news from Dom that I'm going back into the ring, later that evening I get a phone call from Richie. Just from the excitement in the tone of his voice told me that I was about to be given good news.

That was confirmed when Richie told me that he has scheduled a speaking engagement for me at the Trenton State Prison in Trenton, New Jersey.

Rich then went on to say that the superintendent of the prison assured him that there will be anywhere between 500 and 1,000 inmates that will sign up to hear you speak.

I was elated to hear that news and as I began to express to Rich my gratitude for the job that he has done, Rich interrupted me when he said, "Wait Doc, there's more."

Rich then went on to say, "I also have you scheduled to speak at one of the most prestigious private junior high schools in the country, The Blessed Sacred Heart Junior High School of Upper Saddle River, New Jersey.

The next day when the guys came to pick me up to go to the gym, everyone seemed excited. It was easy to notice that Tom and John were excited about hearing the news that I was going to be fighting a young and upcoming fighter.

Rich showed his excitement as he was telling Tommy and Luz that he arranged a speaking engagement for me at the notorious Trenton State Prison. He went on to tell the guys about the prestigious junior high school that I was going to speak at.

I then expressed my excitement when I told the guys that I was going tonight with my son and daughter-in-law to see both my granddaughter Gina and my grandson Luke, both in the finals competing for the New Jersey State Foul Shooting Championship.

Tommy then said, "Naturally you're excited to see your grandkids tonight, but I'm also sure that you're really excited knowing that you'll be fighting a young and upcoming heavyweight."

All the guys were shocked by the answer that was given to Tommy, when I said, "Not really, I don't know how, but somehow, I'm going to win the fight."

I then went on to say, "What I'm nervous about is the thought that one moment I'll be speaking to an audience of convicts in a prison, and the next moment I'll be speaking to a group of sixth, seventh, and eighth graders that come from an affluent environment.

When we arrived at the gym Dom was anxiously waiting for us. It was easy to notice that Dom was excited to prepare me for this fight. Dom expressed to both me and the guys that this will be the test to see if Doc's boxing career continues.

As I began to start my training, Dom was showing me different techniques to use when fighting a guy with his style. My opponents' style is what they call being a southpaw, which means instead of him leading with his left foot and jabbing with his left arm, the fighter does the opposite. He leads with his right foot and throws jabs with his right hand.

I immediately alleviated Dom's concern of my opponent being a southpaw when I said, "He is extremely vulnerable to a right cross."

As that training session continued Dom was becoming more and more annoyed with me for not paying attention to his instructions. That's when I put my arm around Dom and said, "My dear friend, I have plenty more important concerns on my mind at this time, and they do not pertain to boxing."

I have two important speaking engagements scheduled for the week of the fight. I also have to start spending some quality time with my family, starting with me attending my grandchildren competing in a basketball foul shooting competition tonight.

Dom, I'm going to let you in on a secret, my only concern that I have pertaining to the upcoming fight is that I don't seriously hurt my opponent.

I then said to Dom, "I'll make you a deal, get me into better shape and no instructions, I need you to give the instructions to Tommy and Luzzi on how to be trainers and corner men.

I need you to instruct Luzzi that the stool is for me to sit on and rest in between rounds, it's not for him to sit on as he's admiring the models as they're parading around the ring in their skimpy bikinis.

You do what I say, and I promise you that I'll win the fight. Dom started to shake his head with a big smile on his face as we both started to laugh.

Throughout the remainder of the workout Dom's demeanor completely changed, he seemed to loosen up, he was no longer nervous and uptight like when I first walked into the gym.

If I had to bet my money on why the change in Dom's attitude, I would say he bought in completely to what I promised him.

Throughout my entire training session today, Tom, John, and Rich paid no attention to my boring workout. They were not even aware that Dom was annoyed at me for not paying attention to him.

They were pre-occupied with watching this young amateur middleweight as he was sparring in preparation for his first professional fight.

As we were driving back home, I could tell that the guys were really anxious to discuss a business deal with me.

That turned out to be so when Tommy said, "Doc, we were talking to the manager of the middleweight fighter that was doing the sparring today in the gym. He won the AAU National Amateur Championship last year and he's turning pro. He's going to be having his first fight on the same boxing card as you."

Tom then said, "His manager offered us a business deal to buy fifty percent of his stocks for fifty-grand. His manager says he's going to be a champion. We were able to see that he's a really good fighter after watching him spar. The three of us are thinking about investing in him."

As I laid my hand upon my forehead I said, "Oh my God, Lord help me, I'm responsible for these knuckleheads." Talking to myself, I said, *"All of a sudden these guys think they're experts in boxing, sweet Lord, you see, you guys have me talking to myself!"*

I then said in a stern voice, 'The three of you old farts all became grandfathers in recent years, enjoy your grandkids. Your wives will never forgive me if I'm responsible for getting you involved in a long-term boxing venture."

The mission that you're on with me will only take a year and you're all going to be part of winning the boxing heavyweight championship.

By the time I made that last comment, it was time to be dropped off. I said to the guys, "I'm going to be with my grandkids tonight, I'll see you guys tomorrow."

When I entered my son's home the family was having dinner. Amy had cooked a meatloaf, baked potatoes, string beans, and a tossed salad.

My granddaughter, Gina, had everything on her plate and she appeared to be really enjoying her dinner while my grandson, Luke, was eating pastina out of a small bowl.

When I asked Amy, "Does Luke not like meatloaf," my son, Brian, replied, "He likes meatloaf, but he wants to eat light before the contest."

After dinner, we still had an hour before we were going to be heading to the Fairleigh Dickerson University Arena where the tournament was being held.

During this time, I was observing both kids. Luke was going about his preparation like he was about to play in the NBA Championship. He was in deep meditation and concentration on the event.

Gina was listening to her music and talking to her girlfriends on the phone like the contest didn't even exist. It appeared to me that Gina had a much greater concern on what outfit she was going to wear for school tomorrow than any concern about a foul shooting contest. I must say, the comparison between the two really cracks me up.

When we entered the gym, I was completely surprised to see such a large crowd, there was standing room only. We were lucky that Amy's family saved us seats.

The way things turned out was that even before the contest began, I started to give thanks to my SOURCE, my God if you prefer, that destiny has allowed me to be present for this wonderful sporting event.

When the evening ended, Kenny and I were the two proud grandfathers of two New Jersey State Foul Shooting Championships. Gina in her age group for the girls, and Luke in his age group for the boys.

After the kids were awarded their trophies, the entire family went to celebrate by eating hamburgers and fries at the Golden Arches.

The next day when the guys came to pick me up for my workout, I was excited to boast about how well my grandkids performed the night before in their basketball competition. I was proud to tell the guys that they both won the championships.

I was even more proud to say that they play sports with fairness and integrity the way their father played and now teaches as a high school coach.

I then became a little emotional when I thought back to when my mom and dad came to see their grandson, my son, play basketball. He brought them such joy, especially when he would score a basket and as he was running down the court, how he would be looking out the corner of his eye to see if they were watching.

He was a natural, it's like he was born to be on a basketball court, he played with such passion. He went on to be both a hall of fame high school and college ballplayer. He even made second team All American NANI for small colleges.

When we arrived at the gym, I was all fired-up, perhaps it was from my reminiscing as we were driving over that ignited the fuse inside of me.

All I know is that my emotions were all stirred up, so I went to Dom and even though I was not scheduled for sparring that day, I insisted that Dom set me up with some rounds of sparring.

Dom granted my wish by setting me up to spar three rounds, one round each, with three different heavyweights.

When the bell rang for the first round, I came out slow, moving, but throwing no punches. I was concentrating on blocking the peppering right jab being thrown at me.

Dom had previously informed me that the opponent I will be fighting will be throwing many jabs. I was told that his entire offense comes off his jab.

When I threw my first left-right combination my sparring partner went crashing to the canvas. It was then that I realized that the super-natural strength was within me.

So, I then began to throw nothing but cream puff punches the remainder of the round.

The second round I was going against a different sparring partner so my first punch that I threw I didn't completely hold back the force of my punch that resulted in him immediately going down to one knee in pain.

At that point, I was aware that this special strength has stayed within me. So, throughout the remainder of the second round and also the third round, I did nothing but pitter-patter on offense as I practiced my defense.

The next two weeks went by really fast and before I knew it there was only one day before the fight and tonight, I'm scheduled to speak to the inmates at Trenton State Prison.

Ironically, I'm scheduled to speak to the junior high school 9:00 a.m. tomorrow morning the day of the fight. I'm also scheduled to be in Atlantic City tomorrow at 12:30 p.m.

for the weigh-in and physical which is a two-hour car ride away.

With the assumption that I will be speaking at the school to the adolescents for a couple of hours, there is no way that I'm going to be able to make it to the weigh-in and physical that is being held in Atlantic City.

The problem is if I don't show up on time for the weigh-in and physical the State Boxing Commission will cancel my fight.

Dom was begging me to cancel the speaking engagement, rather than have me cancel the fight. It was then that I had to explain to Dom that my last final purpose in life was to speak to as many people as I can to bring forth the message from "Beyond the Beyond."

I then told Dom, "The only interest that I have in boxing at this time is to be able to receive recognition for the sole purpose of my word being heard by many."

The dilemma that we were all facing was rectified when Tommy had his friend offer to transport all of us by his private helicopter from Teterboro Airport to Atlantic City.

After we estimated that the ride from the school to the airport was less than a half-hour, we were assured that our dilemma had been resolved.

Being that it was not necessary for Dom to attend my talk at the prison tonight, we made arrangements for him to be the first to be picked up by Tommy's limo driver tomorrow morning.

The driver will then go to pick up Tommy and then the rest of us.

By the time all five of us are in the limo headed to the school, we will still have plenty of time to assure we will not be late.

After we arranged those plans with Dom, we all said goodbye to him and then we were off, headed to Trenton State Prison.

After a two-hour trip we pulled up to the city of Trenton, scheduled to speak at 8:00 p.m., we had plenty of time to spare so we went to go eat at an Italian pizzeria.

The guys all started to laugh when I ordered a large pizza just for myself. Luzzi then made the comment, "Doc, you're lucky Dom is not here, he would go nuts seeing you eating an entire large pizza the night before your fight."

My answer to Luzzi was, "That's why I'm not getting sausage, pepperoni, olives, peppers, and onions on it because it's the night before the fight."

Everyone started laughing at that explanation before Richie said, "I can't believe that you could eat at all. I would think that you would be too nervous to eat knowing that you're going to be speaking shortly at the notorious Trenton State Prison."

Before I had a chance to answer Rich, Luzzi jumped in by saying, "How could you ask a question such as that, why would Doc be nervous to speak in front of a group of convicts when he's not nervous to go into the ring with a young 220 pound man that is capable of easily killing a man of his age, the answer is easy because he's nuts!"

After we all laughed from John's comment, I responded to Richie's question when I said, "Richie, Richie, Richie, how soon we forget that I lived amongst the toughest, baddest, convicts for seven years in the New York prison system, and I assure you that didn't affect my appetite.

It was now time to enter the prison, all the procedures were all new to Richie and me, but for Tommy and Luzzi, after years of visiting me, they were quite familiar with the prerequisites that were needed before being able to enter the prison as a visitor.

After entering the facilities, we were greeted by two white shirt captains. They were cordial as they escorted us to the backstage of the auditorium.

It was then that the heavyset captain said to us, "You'll be speaking to a standing-room only crowd." After hearing that comment, I took a peek after slightly moving the curtain, what I was observing were 1,000 occupied seats and at least fifty inmates standing at the far end of the auditorium.

There appeared walking on to the backstage a slender tall man that looked to be in his early sixties that introduced himself to us as Mr. Burns, deputy superintendent of the prison.

He then asked if I would like him to introduce me, I replied, as I turned and gently grabbed Richie by the arm and said, "This is my publicist, Richie, he's going to introduce me."

The deputy said, "Very well," as he shook my hand and said, "Good luck." He then turned to Richie and said, "Whenever you're ready" as he walked off the stage.

Richie seemed quite nervous as he came up to me and said, "Doc, what should I say?" I answered him by saying, "I don't know, I don't even know what I'm going to say."

I then said to Rich, "You read my autobiography, pick something to say, now get out there."

Rich walked out onto the stage and said, "Gentlemen of Trenton prison, I would like to introduce you to a man that is one of the forefathers of modern-day physical fitness centers."

"He was a boxing and weightlifting champion and excelled in all sports. He's an inventor of a bodybuilding stopwatch and an author of four bestselling books."

"He's a motivational speaker and he's also a convict. Gentlemen, meet Paul "Doc" Gaccione."

Even before I walked out onto the stage the crowd began to roar from Richie's last words when he called me a convict.

When I walked out onto the stage the crowd continued to applaud for several extra minutes before I began to speak.

The first words that I said were, "Gentlemen, yes I am an ex-con who recently spent seven years at Clinton State Prison of New York before I had my conviction overturned."

I then went on to say, "I have two lifelong dear friends who have accompanied me here tonight. They have just recently started to come hear me speak."

As we were driving over to the prison tonight, my one friend, Johnny, asked me what I was going to speak about to the inmates.

My answer to John was, "I don't have the slightest idea." "The only way that I prepare myself to speak is by asking my SOURCE for the insight to be given to me so that I can have the words to bring forth."

"I tell you in truth if the day comes that the words do not come to me, I promise that you will not hear me speak. In fact, only through the insight that is being given to me am I able to write."

The last six months before my release, I ran into an inmate that has spent the last twenty-nine years incarcerated. It only took a short time before we would start having many long intellectual conversations.

This man was gifted with a special intellect, so I would really enjoy philosophizing with him on deep subject matters.

I remember Nicky asking me this one particular question shortly after we started to have these conversations. "Doc, what are the three most important words to know and use in prison?"

Without hesitation, I said, "Excuse me, please, and thank you." I then added that they are also very important words to always use even in the real world.

Nicky's body language showed that he was surprised that I gave him all three words.

Gentlemen, tomorrow morning I will be speaking to a group of sixth, seventh, and eighth graders at a junior high school in North Jersey. Although I hope to cover a number of subjects with those adolescents, I plan to emphasize to this age group the gift of our imagination.

I say this to you because there are so many people that go through life never recognizing this special gift that is given to all of us.

So, obviously, the sooner that one gets to realize that they have this gift the longer that they could take advantage of it.

"So, I tell you here tonight, when you go later to put your head on the pillow, ask yourself the question, do I realize the gift that I possess?"

The way that I'm going to emphasize one's gift of having an imagination when I speak to those youngsters tomorrow, that's the way that I'm going to put an emphasis on hope and positivity speaking to you tonight.

There is no doubt that it was part of your destiny that brought you here to prison the same way that it was part of my destiny that had brought me to prison.

I tell you in truth that it is also part of your destiny that had you choose to sign-up to hear me speak tonight. I say this to you the same way that it is part of my destiny that brought me here to speak to you tonight.

It was also part of my destiny during the seven years of my incarceration to be given the insight to have published four books while I was also spending countless hours mentoring inmates.

My message to the inmates was that we could always take bad and turn it into good. Life is too precious to waste one single day.

Despite your physical restrictions, your mind is capable of going anywhere that you would like to take it.

I made the inmates that were fortunate enough not to have extremely long sentences aware they could spend much of their time preparing for their future.

I also made the long-timers and lifers realize that there is so much that they could accomplish to make their life meaningful and rewarding.

All the inmates, regardless of their circumstances, were able to recognize what a special gift it is to be alive.

Because prisons permeate negativity, not only did I motivate and inspire the inmates, I also taught them techniques on how to self-motivate.

I let the inmates know that we are all vulnerable to periodically slip into a depressive state; this is a fact even in the outside world.

With some, it occurs quite often within the same day, with others it could be once a day, or once a week or perhaps once a month.

Nevertheless, it's advantageous for one to have the awareness and the knowledge to be able to self-motivate.

When I first started to mentor inmates at Auburn and Clinton Prisons, it was so clear to see within the inmates' eyes, as they began to open so wide and then started to glitter, you could see that it was all from receiving hope.

Due to the negative atmosphere, it was so easy to see that the inmates needed to be nourished with encouragement.

After seeing how inspired inmates were becoming after being motivated and shown how they could make their time meaningful while being incarcerated, it had confirmed to me that by setting up a motivational program in each State Prison would be most advantageous and benefit countless inmates.

So, I'm here tonight to inform you that I'm planning to propose such a program to both the State of New Jersey and New York. I hope to eventually implement this program to all the State Prisons of the land.

I continued speaking to the Trenton audience giving them important messages, such as the importance of always having positivity throughout your life.

Of course, I mentioned Doc's Five Ingredients for Success in Life and I elaborated on the importance of each one.

The crowd applauded when I said that each inmate that attended this gathering tonight will be receiving all four of my books.

I then became emotional when I said to the audience, "I now am going to be speaking privately to each one of you when I say that my entire life has been destined to be nothing less than a phenomenon.

So, tonight I tell you in truth, that just by you entering my path, you are able to change the path of your destiny in whatever direction you choose it to go.

May the SOURCE of the universe, let's call it God, bless all of you, Thank You!

After walking off the stage, Tommy came up to me all excited as he was saying, "Doc listen, they're still applauding."

Even before Luzzi or Richie could comment, Mr. Burns, the Department Super, came up to me and thanked me for coming. I also thanked him for the opportunity to speak before I assured him that someone will be delivering 4,200 of my books for the inmates.

At the time that Richie was making the arrangements with the prison for me to speak, he also had someone at the prison read all four of my books so that they could be approved for distribution.

After speaking for two hours, by the time we left the prison and were heading back home, it was 10:30 p.m. We were now facing an almost two-hour ride to get back up north.

By the time I actually went to bed, it was already 1:00 a.m. Unfortunately, the next morning at 7:00 a.m.; I had to be out of bed and getting ready for the guys to pick me up.

I was scheduled to speak at 9:00 a.m., so we had to be at the school at least a half-hour ahead of time.

As I rushed to shower, shave then get dressed, I was already feeling tired, and the day had not yet begun. Not to mention that tonight I'm going to be having this young, strong, 220-pound muscular professional fighter looking to scatter my brains.

The timing was perfect, as soon as I became ready to leave, is exactly when the limo pulled up. We now had the complete entourage together, Tom, John, Rich, me, and even Dom.

As we were driving over to the school, Dom asked me how I was feeling, I told him that I was feeling a little tired, I didn't get much sleep. That's when Dom started to curse, "Son of a bitch, I knew you should have canceled these damned speaking engagements."

I responded to Dom's comment by saying, "Dom, I'll be honest with you, I fear speaking to these youngsters, after facing them it will be easy to step into the ring with that tough guy."

When we arrived at the school, I had Rich do the introduction between us and Dr. Bell, the principal and his administrative staff.

I couldn't put my finger on it, but there was something about the atmosphere in the hallways that made you feel like this was not your normal junior high school.

When Rich introduced me to the student body of approximately 450 boys and girls, he gave me the same introduction as the night before at the prison, with the exception that he left out being an ex con.

As I started to walk toward the podium my legs began to tremble, and my jaw started to quiver. I then grabbed the top of the podium putting one hand on each side as I began to speak in a really high pitch tone of voice, "Good morning, boys and girls," I continued to speak in that really high pitch voice as I then said, "If I sound like the tooth fairy it's because I'm quite nervous speaking in front of a young group of intellects that will shortly be the future of our country and mother earth."

That comment being said in that high pitch brought laughter from the group.

In my own voice, I said, "Last night I spoke to an audience of over 1,000 inmates at Trenton State Prison and my legs never began to shake the way they are now shaking."

That statement brought much laughter from the audience.

I too attended a parochial school, Sacred Heart Grammar School of Lyndhurst, New Jersey. I mentioned this because there was an incident that took place while I was in the eighth grade that I will never forget.

We had this really strict nun, Sister DeLourdes. One day I was fooling around during class when she came to me and took me by the shoulders and started shaking me like a blender would make an ice cream milkshake.

Sister DeLourdes then stared into my eyes with her piercing scary look that would even frighten the devil himself. She then said in a stern tone of voice, "You're not going to amount to anything more than pushing a broom."

She said those words so forcefully and convincing that she really scared me, growing up I never forgot those words.

Then one day in my early twenties after putting together successful health and physical fitness centers, I became one of the modern-day forefathers of physical fitness.

I could so clearly remember how proud I was as I sat back in my big desk chair and admired the beauty of my elaborate and ornate office that was fashioned in red and gold.

It was then that I thought of the nun at that very moment and I looked up and said to myself, *"WOW!" "I sure showed you, Sister DeLourdes, I built a multi-million-dollar company without a quarter and I never pushed a broom."*

Then through bad habits, I started to get into some trouble. My first situation of being incarcerated was a four-month work release program.

The first day that I went to report, the officer handed me a broom as he said, "Go sweep the day room." I took the broom, walked to the day room when I took the first step to sweep, I thought of the nun, I looked up and said, "I guess you were right, Sister DeLourdes." That brought a chuckle from the group.

When I make arrangements to speak, I truly am not sure what I will talk about, it's the same as when I pick up a pen to write, whatever insight is given to me is the topic of the day.

Although what I say happens to be true, knowing that I was coming this morning to see you, I made sure that I would cover one topic in particular and that is your imagination.

Why I put such a high importance on that particular subject to a group like yours is because you are at a stage in your life where you're searching for what you would like your future to be and what you would like to achieve out of life.

It's so important for you to be aware that throughout life before anyone was able to create or achieve any endeavor, they had to first imagine it in their mind.

I continued speaking about the wonderful gift that we all have, but few people recognize the gift of IMAGINATION.

I spent a sufficient amount of time on the subject knowing how important it was going to be to the students.

After seeing how motivated and inspired the student body had become after recognizing that they have this special gift, I was satisfied that I fulfilled my purpose to them.

Of course, I spent some time covering "Doc's Five Ingredients for Success in Life" before I finished up with the message that I received from "Beyond the Beyond."

I finally finished up by informing the students that each one of them will be receiving all four of my books. That brought overwhelming applause from the student body.

By the time I completed speaking there was very little time to say good-bye to Dr. Bell and his staff.

Most important to me was that Dr. Bell expressed that he was very pleased and impressed. He said that he hasn't seen anyone take over the student body so effortlessly as he'd seen me take command of their attention while motivating and inspiring them.

After saying good-bye, we were off rushing to get into the limo so that we could get to the Teterboro Airport where the helicopter was waiting for us.

ᑫᔐᑫChapter Sevenᕳᐁ

During the trip to the airport, after seeing the expression on Dom's face, Tommy commented, "Dom, you look like you're mesmerized over something." Dom replied, "I'm completely surprised at the impact that hearing Doc speak had on me."

Hearing Dom's comment, all the guys started laughing; Dom then said in an angry tone of voice, "What's so funny?" That's when Luzzi said, "The first time I listened to Doc speak to an audience I thought I was hallucinating." The guys all started laughing from that comment.

Tommy then said to Dom, "We were all surprised the first time we heard Doc speak to an audience." Even I started laughing after that comment.

When we pulled up to the airport, Tommy's friend, George, was patiently waiting for us. It was then that I realized that some time ago, I had dinner with George, Tommy, and all of George's Greek friends at the Sands Casino in Atlantic City.

George was a restaurant czar owning over forty diners throughout Jersey and Tommy used to insure all of them, that's how they became close friends.

At first, Richie was skeptical about getting into the helicopter after hearing the roar of the blades as they were spinning so fast that you were unable to see them. They also caused a lot of wind that could be scary to some.

Nevertheless, Luzzi was able to talk Richie into getting into the aircraft and we were off to Atlantic City.

Within thirty-five minutes we were descending into Atlantic City Airport. To our surprise, there was a limo waiting to take us for the ten-minute ride to the Resorts Hotel and Casino.

We were planning on taking a taxi when we arrived at A.C., but George was thoughtful to have his private limo waiting for us.

When we arrived at the hotel and our entire entourage entered the showroom where they were holding the weigh-in and physicals, we were all shocked to see how large the news media group was waiting for me.

It appeared to all of us that I was getting more attention from the news media than the main event.

At that moment something came over me and I decided to play around, have some fun and take advantage of all the publicity that I was getting.

I guess you could say that I was getting a flashback to Muhammad Ali who I loved and was my boxing idol.

So, as I was walking to the dressing room to get undressed and put on my boxing trunks, I kept saying, "Here comes the champ, the champ is walking."

As I left the dressing room to be weighed-in and get my physical, I kept saying repeatedly, "Here comes the champ, the champ is walking."

That stirred up the news media, not only seeing an old man getting ready to go into the ring in only hours away but to be so brash as to call himself the champ really got their attention.

After I passed the physical, Dom stepped in and would not allow any of the press around me. It was now time to get checked into our rooms and rest.

George surprised us again by getting two of the top penthouses in the hotel, each penthouse had four bedrooms. We now had Tommy, Luzzi, Richie, Dom, George and me in our entourage.

As I was lying on the bed in my room watching the CNN news and trying to rest, Dom came into my room and said, "The promoter came to see me; he told me that because of all the publicity that you're getting, he changed the arrangement of when you're going to fight."

"Instead of you being the first fight of the night, you're now going to be the fight right before the main event."

Dom waiting to hear a comment from me, I angrily started yelling, "Those Republican Senators and Republican politicians have no balls, they have no guts, they're putting their job and party before the loyalty of their country."

"It's so obvious, all the lies, all the illegal things that the President has done despite the overwhelming evidence, and yet there are Republicans that turn their heads because they are scared of losing their job."

"Our forefathers set up the greatest Nation ever on earth. Men have sacrificed their blood and life for the principles of our country and that no man is above the law"

"It took great men such as our forefathers to write the Declaration of Independence and the Constitution so that we can be the greatest nation on earth."

"We have protected ourselves from the President destroying us if he was too powerful, corrupt, or mentally insane through our checks and balances. We protect ourselves through three branches of government, that no man is above the law. The question is, do we have the politicians that are brave enough to follow the laws of our Constitution?"

I was getting ready to continue because I was so infuriated until Dom started yelling at me, "Calm down, you crazy man, you need to rest, you have a fight in a few hours."

As he was shaking his head, he was saying, "You're worried about what the President of the United States is doing when there is a tough guy getting ready to take your head off in a few hours. Get some rest," as he slammed the door.

It seemed like only minutes after Dom slammed the door I crashed out. I finally woke up from the banging on the door. It was Tommy and Luzzi asking me if I just got up, I said yes.

They then both started laughing when they said that earlier Dom came walking down to the casino where we were playing blackjack. He was complaining to us that you were worried about the President being insane, rather than being concerned about the fight, they then started laughing.

Tommy then said Dom wants us to tape your hands; we're getting close to fight time. As Luzzi was taping my one hand, I guess he felt like a trainer because he said to me, "Don't forget to keep your right hand up to block his jab," and I told Luzzi, "Don't forget to bring the stool into the corner when the bell rings to end the round." We all started laughing.

Chapter Eight

When it was time to leave the dressing room, we all looked good. Tommy, Luzzi, and Dom in their cherry-red silk with white lettering training jackets, and me with my white satin robe and trunks with red trim and lettering.

As we entered the ring the noise of the crowd was deafening. After seeing the TV cameras, I was reminded that the fight was being shown on cable TV.

After meeting in the middle of the ring for instructions from the referee, my opponent towered over me by three to four inches, his physique was a sculpture of nothing but muscle.

When the bell rang for the first round to start, I went toward him. I felt the first of his jabs crashing into my forehead. Before I had a split-second to think, there was another stiff jab hitting me between my eyes, I said to myself, *"Holy shit this hurts."*

I then thought of what Luzzi said. I put my right hand up high and I started to be able to block his jab. I then started to dance a little, but he put pressure on me, so I had to throw a few punches to keep him off me.

After I threw a few left hooks and right crosses, I knew I didn't possess any special strength entering my punch.

Just the normal strength and power of my punch was good enough to keep him off me, at least for the rest of round one.

As I was walking back to the corner after the bell rang, I was saying to myself, I have to find a way to get emotional so that I can get the super strength to enter my body.

When I got to the corner and sat on the stool as Dom was putting Vaseline on my face, and Luzzi was taking out my mouthpiece, Tommy said to me, "Doc, your son Brian is here, he's sitting in the VIP section, first row with his friends, he came up to me and asked me to stop the fight, he sounded very upset."

After hearing what Tommy said, I got so emotional and I turned to Tommy and said, "Please don't stop the fight, I know what I'm doing."

When the bell rang for the second round, all I could think about was my son being worried that his father could be getting hurt.

As I walked out for the second round all emotional, I had my right hand purposely low, when my opponent threw his stiff crippling jab, I came over his jab with a right cross that missed his jaw but hit the top of his forehead. He went crashing down to the canvas and didn't get up for over five minutes.

When I saw my opponent crashing to the ground, thinking that he might be seriously hurt, I started to hyperventilate to an extent that concerned me that I might get a heart attack.

The crowd was going crazy from what they had just witnessed when the TV announcers rushed up into the ring to speak with me; the noise level was still so loud that I could barely hear their questions.

At that moment I noticed that the doctor had completed examining my opponent, so I told the TV announcers that I will be right back.

I then rushed over to the doctor grabbing him by the shoulders, as I asked, "Doctor, is he going to be ok?" He replied, "He's going to be fine."

Hearing that good news, I became so emotional that I picked the doctor up and started hugging him. After putting him down, I went back to the announcers to answer their questions.

The first question that was asked, "How did you ever get this incredible punching power?" "Rocky Marciano and George Foreman were the two hardest hitting heavyweight fighters of all time and you're twice their age."

My answer to them was, "I eat my spinach, unlike Popeye, I don't eat my spinach out of the can, I prefer it sautéed in oil and garlic over a bed of pasta."

Why do you risk your life at your age of seventy-two by getting into the ring? "I need to get the publicity so that I can become well known."

The one announcer sounded confused as he said, "Are you telling us that you're risking your life simply for the reason of becoming well known?"

"My answer to you is, that is correct, I need to become well known to bring forth a message, when I speak, I need to be heard."

The two TV announcers had puzzlement on their faces after that answer. Dom stepped in and said, "That's it, we have to go back to the dressing room for the doctor to check his blood pressure and heart."

As I began to walk away, the one announcer followed me and then stuck the microphone in my face and said, "are you going to fight again and if so, when?"

I responded to his question, despite Dom telling me to keep walking when I told him, yes, I'm going to fight again next month and every month thereafter until I win the heavyweight championship of the world.

I then went on to say, I have no time to waste, especially at my age, I have to get this boxing career over with really fast, there is still much I need to do.

The announcer then looked like he was going to start foaming at the mouth when he excitedly was yelling, "what do you mean when you say, I have still much to do?" I didn't answer that question; I just kept walking toward the dressing room.

When we arrived at the dressing room the doctor was already there waiting for us. It was a fast exam, blood pressure, heart rate, eyes, pulse, balance. This was not mandatory; it was what Dom wanted for safety reasons.

By the time the doctor completed his exam, my son, Brian, and my nephew, John, walked into the room with all their friends. Most of these guys were like my Godsons. They lined up to congratulate me and give me a hug.

It was Michael, Eddie, Robin, Stevie, Nicky and Nick, Joe Tondi, Sean, Danny and Billy. Brian even brought his father-in-law and brother-in-law, Kenny and Todd with him.

"Happy to see everyone," I said, "I wish that I could take all of you to the steakhouse. As soon as I said those words, Tommy's friend George stepped up again and said,

"I'm going to immediately have a private party room set up for a count of twenty-five guests for a steak dinner, you are all invited.

That brought a roar throughout the dressing room that made me say, "Wow, I didn't get that reaction after winning the fight!" Everyone in the crowded dressing room started laughing.

The night turned out great, everyone ate like kings, the best aged steaks that money could buy, and all had many, many laughs.

The next morning when I woke up, I walked into the living room of our suite, Luzzi and Richie were up having coffee and both reading the paper. Dom, Tommy, and George were still sleeping.

Before either one of them asked if I wanted coffee, they both said, you're all over the paper. I then said, Luz, please pour me a cup of Joe. Luzzi then said, "You're not hearing me, I mean you're all over the paper, not just the sports pages."

Richie then said, "You're on the front page of the Asbury Press, you also have a story written about you in the main section of their paper."

John then said, Doc, wait till you hear this one, the State doctor that checked your opponent last night after the fight, and then assured you that he was alright, that doctor was sent to the hospital in the middle of the night.

They discovered that he has two fractured ribs and two broken bones in each arm. The hospital report said that his entire upper body was bruised and black and blue.

The doctor claims that when he told you that the other fighter was going to be ok, you became so emotional that you wrapped your arms around his arms and then picked him up and began to hug him, the doctor said that's when the injuries occurred.

When the other guys woke up, Luzzi, Rich, and I hung out in the living room suite with them while room service was bringing them their breakfast.

Richie then started telling Dom, Tommy and George what Luzzi and he had read in the newspapers about the fight last night.

Luzzi then jumped in and said that the fight doctor claimed that when Doc picked him up and hugged him in the ring after the fight, Doc fractured the doctor's ribs and broke bones in the doctor's arms.

Luzzi went on to say, "The New York Post has coined Doc, "The grandpa superman."

I responded to Luzzi's comment by saying, "That same newspaper, the New York Post, had also coined me with the name, "The Godfather of Souls" when they did a featured story on me and the first book that I had penned, "Beyond the Beyond," my journey to destiny. The New York Post put that story out on Easter Sunday.

Luzzi then said, "I would say that the publicity Doc is looking for is just about to start happening."

Hearing Luzzi's comment, I responded by saying, "Rich, you're my public relations man; you are going to be in charge of handling the newspaper and TV news media."

All my comments are going to be coming through you; I'm not going to be speaking to the news media until I have completed my objective through boxing.

Till then Rich, you're going to be my voice. Luzzi started to laugh as he said, "Good luck Rich, the news media are like leeches, if they want a story, they will suck your blood to get it."

After everyone had completed eating breakfast, we started getting ready to head back home to North Jersey.

My first thought was, *Shit; I hate that two-hour ride to get back home until I realized that we were going back in George's helicopter to Teterboro Airport, which was only a stone throw from home.*

When we arrived at Teterboro, there were both Tommy and George's limousines waiting for us. Before George left us, I thanked him for everything that he had done, and let him know how sincerely I appreciated his generosity.

After giving him a big hug, I said to him, "I tell you in truth when the time comes that I'll be fighting for the championship, you will be my special guest." George's response was, "I'll be honored to be there."

After everyone said good-bye to George, we all entered Tommy's limo. Usually, I'm the first to be dropped off because we're always coming from south to north.

Today, being that we're headed from north to south, Tommy is going to be the first to be dropped off.

As we approached Tommy's home, his wife, Bernadette, was anxiously standing in the front of her house waiting for the limo to pull up. When we arrived, all of us exited the limo to say hello to Bern.

Bern approached me first with a kiss and congrats for winning the fight. She then went to Luzzi with a kiss as she said to him, "John, you and Tommy looked good on TV wearing those beautiful candy apple red silk jackets."

"You guys really looked like you knew what you were doing." That's when I jumped in and said, "Bern, let's not get crazy." Everyone started laughing.

Tommy then introduced both Richie and Dom to his wife. I then said to Bern, "Being that I don't want you or Maryann to get mad at me, I'm going to make arrangements for both of you to come to my next fight."

No longer than ten minutes had passed after dropping Tommy off when Dom's cell phone started to ring, it was the promoter from Resorts Hotel and Casino.

He's asking Dom if I would be interested in signing a contract for the next four fights to be held and promoted at Resorts Hotel and Casino in Atlantic City.

Dom's response to the offer was, "I'm with the fighter now, we're on our way home. We'll discuss the offer and get back to you."

After Dom explained the situation to me, Luzzi immediately jumped into the conversation by saying, "Doc, you're becoming red hot, you're in demand even though you only have had two fights. So, God only knows how far the news media is going to go with your story."

Luzzi continued on, "The promoter is starting to get the feedback from the news media on the potential of the money that could be made from the novelty of you being an old man."

After hearing Luzzi's comments, I turned to Dom and said, "John is completely correct." I then said to Dom, "I want you to call the promoter back with this offer."

"I will sign a contract for a four-fight deal with Resorts Hotel and Casino provided that the fights are one month apart."

"This agreement is contingent on only if I don't get seriously cut or injured whereby I'm unable to get back into the ring in such a short time as one month."

I then instructed Dom to let the promoter know that you have to agree with who my four opponents will be.

Hearing my last demand, Dom responded, "Is that it?" Luzzi immediately jumped in again and said to me, "What about the money, you're now becoming in demand?" Again, I said to Luzzi, "You're right!"

I turned to Dom and said, "Tell the promoter that I want double the purse that I received for last night's fight for the first of the four fights. I then want double of that purse for each separate remaining fight."

Luzzi then said to Dom, "Make sure the promoter understands that it's double the purse for each of the four separate fights." Dom then said, "What you're trying to say is that each fight the purse gets doubled." "Yeah, that's correct, you got it right," was Luzzi's comment.

Rich sounded completely confused when he asked me the question, "Why Doc is it so important that those four fights have to be only one month apart?"

I responded to everyone when I said, "Well fellas if I lose any fight, my boxing journey is over. If I keep winning, I still don't have any time to waste because there is still so much, I need to accomplish before I have fulfilled my purpose in life."

If I win the heavyweight championship of the world, an incredible feat, that will be only a stepping stone on the road to my final destiny.

I wrote a story on Muhammad Ali for a learning lesson that I was giving to a young black kid at Auburn Prison. I later put this story in my book, "The Godfather of Souls." I don't know if any of you recollect the story and the message.

So, I told Rich to ask the limo driver if my books were in the limo. The driver replied to Rich, "The left compartment under the middle seat has all four of Doc's books.

Throughout my entire talk to Puna on Ali, he didn't say a word, he just listened intensely. When I was finished talking, he responded, "Wow, he was quite a man!" He went on to say that he had no idea that he was such an important figure in helping the black man in his fight for equality and self-respect. "I can see that he helped the black man to be proud of being black."

I replied, "That is correct, Puna, that's what Ali did with his beliefs and courage, and it's important that you can see that. He made many black people see that they weren't second class citizens and that they should be proud of who they are. He also made many white people see the importance of this happening at that time in American history. He risked everything; fame, fortune, his title, livelihood, and even his life for his beliefs."

After asking Rich to get me my book, The Godfather of Souls, Rich opened the compartment and handed me the book.

I then said to the guys, I would like to read to you what I wrote about Mohammad Ali, and then perhaps you will be able to see where I'm coming from. Richie then responded by saying, "Ok Doc, let it rip." I then began to read.

Puna replied, "I'm going to get my pad to take notes."

I began our lesson by saying, "We're going to be talking about the greatest heavyweight boxing champion, Mohammad Ali. I chose him for today's discussion not because of his remarkable boxing career, but because destiny led him to be an important man in world history."

Mohammad Ali was my boxing hero. Part of that reason was that I had hopes of becoming the heavyweight boxing champion. The other reason was that I had such great admiration for his discipline, determination, perseverance and confidence.

He had such belief in himself that he could will his destiny and he did. As extraordinary an athlete as he was, that's not the reason I chose to bring him up for discussion.

The reason I brought him up is that his destiny led him to far greater things than being heavyweight champion of the world. It was his beliefs and convictions, his courage to endure persecution that helped change racism and injustice in America. He helped to give self-pride to the black race.

It was his destiny to become a leader to the black Americans at a time in American history where it was so desperately needed. He had the courage to refuse to be inducted in the Army not only because of his religious beliefs, but also because he felt it was wrong to go fight for freedom in a foreign land when he and his people were not truly given freedom, equality, and justice here in his own land of America.

He was guaranteed by the Army that he would not have to go to war. He was promised that all he would do was go on tours and box exhibition fights. He risked going to jail, was stripped of his title, was barred from making a living from his profession, and lost most of his popularity from white America, all because of his beliefs and principles.

There was a time when he was the most recognizable figure on planet earth. His name was better known than any world leader of his time. Here was a man that was disgraced, persecuted, and his livelihood taken away from him in the prime of his life. He faced death threats, but he wouldn't waver from his beliefs and convictions. Here he was so close to spending five years of his life in prison, yet destiny had him years later being awarded the Medal of Honor, presented to him by the President of the United States in the White House.

Yes, he was destined to become the world heavyweight champ, but he was also destined to become such a monumental figure for mankind.

It was almost an impossibility to beat Sonny Liston and win the heavyweight championship of the world, but it was destined to be. It was almost an impossibility to be able to win back the heavyweight championship from George Foreman, but it was all destined to be.

Destiny had him come at a time in American history where he was truly needed to help pave the way to give his people self-pride. His self-pride was a perfect way to be an influence on giving his people self-pride in themselves.

"I brought up Mohammad Ali to make you aware, that here was a man who was just a boxer, a man that was far from being perfect, yet through his beliefs and courage, destiny had him have an impact on helping change the world."

I tell you in truth Puna, you have to have a purpose in life for your life to have meaning. For you to have your dreams come true, you have to dream. To achieve your goals, you must have goals.

That's our discussion for today.

As soon as I completed reading the story that I had written on Ali, Dom was the first to comment when he said, "Doc, boxing has been part of my entire life."

I would also like to think that I'm very well informed on the history of the top fighters, and also the history of the sport of boxing, yet sadly, even though I knew of Ali's boxing greatness and his illustrious boxing career, I never really realized the impact that he had on mankind.

My response to Dom's comment was, "Even sadder than that, most black Americans are unaware of the impact that Ali had on men."

Rich then said, "Doc, telling that story has not just enlightened about Ali's remarkable life, but I also see why you told that story in respect to yourself. I'm able to clearly see that your boxing endeavor is just a small part of the life portrait that you're trying to paint of your life."

By the time Richie completed his statement, the limo was pulling up to my son's home. Being that we were all taking tomorrow off, I said good-bye to the guys, "I'll see you all the day after tomorrow."

As I was getting out of the limo, I reminded Luzzi to send my love to his wife, Maryann.

When I walked into the house, I heard a voice coming from the den saying, "Bri is that you?" I responded to my daughter-in-law, Amy's question by saying, "Brian won't be home for another hour, I'm here because we took a helicopter," as I was walking into the den.

After Amy saw that the voice was mine, she came over excitedly to hug and congratulate me on the fight. She told me that all her friends came over to watch the fight on TV.

She said, "Your grandkids, Luke and Gina, were so excited to see you on TV." That's when I stopped and thought for a moment, how much that meant to me.

Amy was putting this raspberry cream frosting on a cake that she said she baked for me to celebrate the victory.

Amy then said, "go lie down, when the kids come home from basketball practice and Brian gets home, I'll wake you for supper."

I was in a sound deep sleep when I was awakened by having two bodies jumping on top of me. They were tickling me at the same time.

Both Brian and Luke, as they were on top of me, were saying, "Let's see how tough you are now?" When I looked up, alongside the bed, I saw Amy and Gina cheering for me, they were saying, "come on Grandpa Doc, show them wise guys who's the boss, teach them a lesson."

Once I had reversed the position with Brian and Luke, and now had them both under me, they decided to call for a truce and go eat supper.

ᥴᥬ᠙Chapter Nine᥏᥎

When morning arrived, even before I had my first cup of coffee, my cell phone started to ring, on the other end, sounding like he was foaming from the mouth, was Dom. He started out talking so fast, that I had to stop him and tell him to slow down.

After Dom had gotten his composure, he began to tell me that we were given everything that we had asked for from the promoter. Dom then went on to say that he was also very satisfied with the four opponents that he selected.

Dom felt that the opponent that he selected for the first fight, each fight thereafter, the opponent would be a step up in competition.

After congratulating Dom for making the deal, I asked him to please call Tommy and explain the deal to him. I then told Dom to tell Tommy to pick me up tomorrow at three to go to the gym. I then told Dom that I'll see him tomorrow.

When the next day arrived, three o'clock sharp, the limo pulled up with Tommy, Luzzi, and Richie.

The first thing I said to Tommy was, "did Dom call you last night to fill you in on the deal that we made with Resorts?"

Tommy responded by saying, "Yeah, Dom filled me in," and then I explained the deal to John and Rich as we were driving over to get you."

I told the guys that we have to have a meeting with Dom in his office after today's workout.

After my workout, we all gathered in Dom's office. The first thing I said to the guys was you already know that the next four months of our venture has been already set.

If I win all four of those fights the venture will continue. If I lose any one of the four fights the road to that venture will come to a dead end.

Last night my insight was telling me that I need to go on a sabbatical, I need to start preparing to write my next book.

At that moment you could see that Dom was becoming nervous just from his mannerism. He then asked the question, "Doc, are you telling me that you're not going to fight any of the fights that I scheduled for you?"

"No, no, no, that's not what I'm saying. What I'm saying is that I'm only going to be coming to the gym three times a week, the rest of the time I'm going to be spending in seclusion. I'm going to be on sabbatical for the next four months."

I then turned to Rich, "the only thing that I will take the time for is if you set up any speaking engagements for me."

As I then turned to Tommy and Luz, I let them know how much I needed them. I was hoping that with their sales expertise, and their business connections, they would be able to get big companies to donate money to our cause. That accomplishment would allow us to buy my books to send to all the State prisons.

Luzzi made the first response when he said, "Doc, you keep winning these fights and big companies are going to be looking for you." Tommy then said, "Don't worry, we'll be able to get some companies that need a tax write-off to donate."

So, the next four months were set, as long as I kept winning. I had gone into hibernation and only came out to go to the gym. All the rest of my time was meditating and doing my writing.

The first month of my sabbatical, Richie hadn't scheduled a speaking engagement, so I really didn't go anywhere except for my grandkid's basketball games.

Our four-month game plan nearly came to an end, the first ten seconds of my first of four fights, when as soon as the bell rang, I proceeded to the middle of the ring where I was greeted by a powerhouse straight right cross.

When his fist made contact with my jaw, both my dentures along with my mouthpiece came flying out of my mouth. I immediately dropped to the canvas on one knee, a second later, I found myself on all fours, helpless, trying to get up before the count of ten.

I didn't feel any pain, all I knew was that one moment I was walking to the middle of the ring and then in a flash of a split second I found myself on the canvas trying to get up.

I have no doubt that the extra time that it took for the referee to go fetch my dentures that were still in my mouthpiece, and then the time that it took for the referee to go to the corner to ask Dom to wash the mouthpiece off, gave me the necessary time to be able to clear my head.

Now that my head was clear, I knew better that I should be grabbing him and tying him up into a clinch. When I wasn't doing that I was dancing with my footwork, trying to stay away from his right hand.

When the bell rang to end round one, when I walked to the corner, standing there alongside Dom was Luzzi, white as a ghost. He nervously grabbed me by the shoulders as he called me by my childhood nickname, "T, are you ok?"

I answered him, "who are you?" When I saw how he responded to that question, I said, "Luz, I'm only kidding you." I then sat on the stool and let the guys work on me.

Before the bell rang to start the second round, I already knew that I won the fight because I could feel the super-strength entering my body.

When the bell rang, I went directly to him as I was throwing a left hook to his mid-section. His right arm partially blocked the punch, but my fist still made it to his ribs.

He immediately went to one knee before he went into a fetal position. It was easy to see from the expression on his face the excruciating, agonizing pain that he was enduring.

X-rays taken later at the hospital showed he had a fractured right arm and two fractured ribs.

The fans were going crazy that night after seeing that knockout, and then after the news media had gotten the report from the hospital that my opponent had not only two fractured ribs but also a fractured right arm from trying to block the punch, they ran with that story.

The news media was starting to have a party over the unique story that was developing across the country. Sports reporters and boxing experts were even starting to mention the old man wonder, "Grandpa Doc" with the likes of Marciano, Foreman, and Tyson.

Now that this story of the old man, Grandpa Doc, was starting to catch on with interest and popularity, and being that I had gone into seclusion, the news media was now starting to be all over Dom, Tommy, Luzzi, and Richie.

When the second month came along, the second fight of the four-fight deal was no different than the first. The old man's opponent was sprawled out on the canvas before being taken to the hospital.

During the second month, Rich had scheduled two speaking engagements for me. The first was a County Jail, and the second, believe it or not, was a writer's seminar. I found it very interesting the response and feedback that I received from that group of people.

I was very pleased, and I felt that both appearances went exceptionally well; that was very important to me.

When the third month rolled in and it was time for the third fight of the four-fight contract the popular demand had become so big that even despite my only having a four and no loss record, Resorts had to move the fight from their 3,000 seat showroom in the hotel to the 19,000 seat Atlantic City Convention Center.

The fight was sold out the first day that tickets went on sale.

Even though this was going to be only my fifth professional fight, because of the overwhelming interest of the public the promoter made my fight the co-featured main event of the evening.

I guess you could say the boxing fans were not disappointed, despite only thirty seconds had gone by in the first round when both my opponent and I simultaneously threw a right-hand punch.

His punch landed on the top of my forehead while my punch landed square on his jaw having his mouthpiece go flying into the air as his body was descending to the canvas.

Later that night I was told that my opponent's mouthpiece landed right on George Foreman's lap, who was sitting in the front row.

My response after hearing that was, "I really love George Foreman, I think he's a good man."

I was also completely surprised to hear that there were a few other great champions at the fight along with a few celebrities.

The news media was taking this even greater and further than my insight had told me.

The next morning, Dom, Tom, John, Rich, and I went to one of the hotel restaurants for breakfast before heading back up North.

After we all gave our order to the waiter, Dom said he had an announcement to make. As I looked at all the other faces at the table, they all showed puzzlement, so I knew that we all were hearing Dom's news for the first time.

Dom then said, "If Doc wins this fourth of four-contracted fights and becomes 6-0, and if he doesn't get seriously hurt in doing so, Caesar's Palace in Las Vegas is going to give him a fight on the undercard of the middleweight championship next month."

Hearing that news, all the guys began to get excited, Luzzi said, "Viva Las Vegas, here we come." Tommy then said, "That's right, we're the top trainers in the world, that's where we belong, in Las Vegas."

Richie then said, "Wow, we're now big time!" He then started to get excited when he thought of all the beautiful girls then said, "Hey, I'm single!"

After completing breakfast and shortly after we all entered the stretch limo, Rich said, "I was trying to hold this news from Doc until tomorrow, but because I'm so excited over Vegas, I'm going to tell him now."

Rich then said to me, "Doc, I have you scheduled to speak at Clinton Correctional Facility in three weeks. I knew how much this would mean to you so I gave it my all to make it happen."

I became so excited and overwhelmed after hearing that news I became a little choked-up hearing that news.

All the other guys also showed excitement after hearing that news, but Dom. Tommy then said to Dom, "What's the matter, you look disappointed?"

Dom responded to Tommy, "everyone is celebrating going to Las Vegas, Doc has to win this fight first, and also not get hurt in doing so. I'm concerned that this speaking engagement just one week away from the fight will be a distraction. This fight is so important, we don't need any distractions."

Rich then said to Dom, "I tried my best to get the speaking engagement scheduled for after the fight. The response that was given to me from the Director of Activities was that this is the only open date on the calendar for this year."

I then jumped in and said, "Rich, you did a great thing, this means so much to me. I tell you all in all truth that you will be seeing that this was all destined to be."

I then promised Dom that my return to Clinton was all in the cards. It will not interfere with the fight.

To everyone's surprise, even though I stood in seclusion for this fourth-fight contract deal, I was training harder and more intense than in the past.

The funny thing is that the guys believed the reason for the increased intensity in my training was from being inspired about the opportunity of going to Vegas.

Truth be told, knowing that I was going to shortly return to Clinton Prison was overwhelming to me. All my concentration, all my thought processes were focused on my speaking engagement to the inmates at Clinton Prison.

Being honest, there was no room in my mind to even think about the fight, but I did do everything to hide that situation from the guys, especially Dom.

Despite Dom complaining that the five-hour trip one way to get to Clinton Prison was too long, he still wanted to make the trip with us. Tommy and Luzzi had made that trip so many times in the past to come visit me, it seemed like they didn't even give it a second thought. As for Rich, he was so excited that he was the one responsible for putting this entire event together, he didn't wasn't at all concerned about the five-hour trip.

When the limo was getting closer to the prison, I was mesmerized seeing those thirty-foot walls with gun towers on top of the walls. I found it interesting that it was so intimidating to me since I had spent six years on the other side of those walls.

This was a fortress, the size of a New York City block that was first constructed in the mid-eighteen hundreds.

As we were going through all the prerequisites to get into the prison, Tommy and Luzzi were telling us ahead of time what to expect next. Perhaps you could say that they were not only showing off to Dom and Richie by also to me.

After we completed all the procedures necessary for entering this compound, when we finally arrived in the back of the stage, the guys were in awe from what they were witnessing.

Not only were there many correctional officers that were entering the back of the stage to say hello, even I was surprised when I saw the number of white shirts and suits coming in to give their best wishes.

When Rich was about to introduce me, here is what he said. "Gentlemen of Clinton, after what I observed from backstage, and knowing the person I'm about to introduce you to was here with you only one year ago, so gentlemen all I have to say is, here's Doc."

When I walked onto the stage I heard the chant of my name begin, Doc, Doc, Doc, it seemed like it went on forever. When it finally stopped, the first word I said to the inmates was "DESTINY!" That brought a great roar from the audience.

I then began to speak, "My brothers and my sons, it was destiny that brought me here to Clinton as an inmate, and it was also destiny that brought me here to be with you tonight."

The many times that I passed by the auditorium while the doors were open, as I walked down this hallway, I knew that one day I would be up here on this stage speaking to all of you.

I have already seen the standing-room only crowd that's at the end of the auditorium.

I have already seen myself up here on stage each time I had passed by this auditorium.

I have also seen all of you sitting here each time I walked by and saw the doors were open.

With every fiber of my being I knew that this time would come. I knew that I would be standing at this very spot of this stage looking upon all of you, bringing forth the message from "Beyond the Beyond."

How do I know this to be true? I know this to be true because it's all part of my destiny.

Your signing up to be here tonight, to hear my words, this is all part of your destiny. Many of you out there have read one, two or possibly all of my books. I know my books are out there throughout the prison.

I'm sure there are many of you out there that have spent many hours with me standing in front of your gate speaking one-on-one to you. That was all destined to be. The question is, was it destined to be for you to hear my words for the purpose of turning your life around, becoming whoever you want to become?

Or is it part of your destiny to be given the key that would open the door to show you the way to be whatever you would like to be, and then you make the choice NOT TO USE THE KEY.

I tell you in truth, you control your fate. Destiny has brought me here to give you the spark, the spark that is necessary to ignite the fire within yourself to get the burning desire to become whoever you wish to become.

I tell you in truth, I can't do any of this for you. I can only bring you the spark. It can only be you to cause the fire inside of you.

I then went on to talk about Doc's Five Ingredients for Success in Life. I reminded the group of the special gift that we all possess and that is your imagination. I made sure that I elaborated on this special gift.

I preached to them that the secret to success in life is to always possess positivity and the secret to happiness in life is to love and believe in yourself.

When I first came to prison, I met a wise old man. He asked me the question, "What are the three most important words that you should know in prison?"

I responded by saying, "That's easy, excuse me, please, and thank you."

Out of nowhere, I began to become extremely emotional, I was actually having a tough time holding back the tears as I was saying to the inmates that coming to Clinton was not just part of my destiny to help inmates, but it was also destined for me to see the many signs that were given to me during my stay here so that I could be reassured of my purpose.

From the very first day that I walked behind these humongous walls, there must have been a guardian angel that jumped on my shoulder.

I then said to the inmates, I want the twenty strongest weight lifters to come up onto the stage. If there is one or more that could beat a seventy-three-year-old man in arm wrestling, I will have 1,000 dollars put into your inmate account.

Turning to the left side of the stage, standing behind the curtain, was the guys. I asked Tommy and Luzzi if they would bring a table and two chairs out onto the stage.

As the guys were bringing out the table and chairs, the muscular inmates were lining up on stage at the same time.

After Tom and John brought out the table, they then both walked back out holding a chair. It was then that Luzzi whispered to me, "Crazy man, what are you doing?" "Dom is going crazy back there; he's foaming from the mouth. He says you're going to injure your arm and blow the fight."

My response to Luzzi was, "Tell Dom to believe in my destiny."

I then said to myself, as I looked at twenty young strongmen, all hungry and excited to win $1,000, *"Oh my God, what did I do, this mistake is going to cost me $20,000.*

Out of nowhere, I became extremely emotional, I could feel the tears as they began to fall down the side of my cheeks as I said to the crowd, "As sure as every word that I said to all of you tonight is destined to be, that is the same way that I will show all of you tonight that it is destiny for this seventy-three-year old man to beat these twenty strong young men in arm wrestling."

I sat at the table and motioned for the first guy to sit; at that moment I could feel this incredible strength entering my body. It was like I was getting fed this incredible strength intravenously.

No longer than ten seconds after the first inmate put his hand in mine, he was defeated. Later on, I was told that after defeating the first inmate, Dom's leg started to buckle, and he almost passed out.

After defeating the first guy, I kept waving for the next inmate to come to the table. As each inmate put their hand into mine, it was only seconds before they were defeated. The crowd was going crazy, they couldn't believe their eyes.

As I was defeating each guy one by one, as they were walking off stage, each one was holding their arm like they were in pain.

After I slammed down the last inmate's arm, I stood up from the table and I said to the audience, "Destiny, never forget my words that I bring to you, your efforts and actions each day influence your destiny. May God bless each and every one of you." I then walked off stage to roaring applause and then the chant began, Doc, Doc, Doc.

When I went backstage all the guys were laughing and fooling around with Dom, actually, they were teasing and breaking Dom's balls for being so nervous.

Luzzi was doing an imitation of Dom's reaction when he heard me say that I was going to arm wrestle the twenty strongest inmates in the audience.

Everyone was hysterical laughing at Luzzi's skit on Dom, he was really funny. After all the guys stopped laughing, Dom asked me if my arm was ok.

I answered Dom by saying, "Do you want to arm wrestle me?" The guys all started laughing again.

After I said good-bye to the top brass that was working that night and thanked them for the hospitality and the invite, we were off to a restaurant and hotel to spend the night.

After getting in the limo, Tom suggested that we go to Plattsburg. It's only a fifteen-minute ride from here and they have a nice Sheraton Hotel there. We could eat right in the hotel's restaurant, the foods not bad.

John re-affirmed Tommy's suggestion when he said, "Yeah, you're right, we stayed there one of the times that we came here to visit Doc."

After checking in, we all went to the restaurant. As we were eating, I almost choked on the food I was eating, when Luzzi said to me in a very suspicious way, "Doc, something is very fishy, where did you get that kind of strength to arm wrestle?" "I remember you always telling me that despite how strong your arms were, you were never good at arm wrestling."

Tommy then said, "Luz, you're right, I remember when we all used to lift weights; Doc saying, "As strong as my arms are, I can't arm wrestle."

Dom then said, "This entire thing doesn't make any sense to me, everything about Doc doesn't make any sense to me. The one thing that I do know is all you guys from Lyndhurst are freaking nuts."

We all started to really laugh after Dom made that comment. I then immediately started to ask Dom questions about my upcoming fight. I was trying to use diversion on Tom and John.

Diverting the guys away from their question was much easier than trying to explain where I got this incredible strength from.

When I went to my hotel room and put my head on the pillow, I started to realize how stupid I was. When I think of the risk that I took challenging the twenty strongest weightlifters in the prison to an arm-wrestling contest, I had to be crazy.

Knowing that I had no guarantee if the super strength was going to enter my body, showed me that I wasn't using my head.

Just the thought that my mistake might have cost me $20,000 makes me shake my head.

As I continued to reminisce about that situation earlier, I realized that my actions risked the most important commitment that I made to the inmates, and that was when I told them that by beating all these strong men in arm wrestling would show all of you that everything I said was destined to be.

The next morning, the way we planned, we all got up early and had a fast, short breakfast. Some had cereal, some just toast or a bowl of oatmeal, besides that we knocked off a pitcher of OJ and two pots of coffee, we then were on our way to get back home.

As we were driving, all the guys were able to see the glow of contentment on my face. Finally, Tommy made a comment, "Doc, you look like you're very pleased with how your visit went at Clinton Prison."

I responded to Tommy's comment by becoming very emotional as I said, "words could not express how I feel after having the opportunity to return to Clinton. Tom, like I said on stage, after walking past that auditorium time and time again, and then to have the premonition that one day I would be up there speaking to the inmates of Clinton. Seeing it become a reality is hard to put into words."

I wanted to also express to Tommy and the rest of the guys that when I first heard that I was going to be speaking at Clinton, I became so excited that I was unable to concentrate on the fight but I decided to keep that thought to myself because I didn't want to irritate Dom anymore.

As we started to get close to my son's house Dom said, "Ok men, we all have to start to focus on the fight, we're going to have only two workouts left in the next few days before we're back on the road to Atlantic City."

Luzzi then said, "WOW!" "We've been so preoccupied that I didn't even realize that the fight is only four days away."

When the limo pulled up to the front of the house, we were ambushed by an army of news reporters as I was getting out of the vehicle.

That's when I turned to the guys and said, "Hey, I have to do the fighting, this is your job fellows, be nice to them" as I rushed past the reporters and into the house.

After two days of training in Dom Bufano's Gym, we were all back on the road heading to Atlantic City. We wanted to be there a day before the fight.

☜Chapter Ten☞

A s we were checking into the hotel I remembered, and then I turned to Tommy and said, "Bernadette and Maryann, I promised them that I would have them come to my next fight, you have to get your limo driver to bring them here tomorrow."

That's when Luzzi jumped in and said, "Don't worry about the girls, our wives decided that they're going to come to the fight next month in Las Vegas."

Hearing what Luzzi said, I replied, "Holy shit!" I now even have pressure on me from your wives, if I don't win this fight tomorrow night, there will be no Vegas.

The day of the fight, even though the fight was being held at the Atlantic City Convention Center just like the last fight, thanks to me, nevertheless, the weigh-in and physical were being held at the Resorts Showroom.

At noon, as we were walking down to the showroom for the weigh-in, we overheard that the showroom was packed with sports reporters.

At that moment, something came over me and I decided to play around and do a skit the way Ali once did. I did that skit at the last weigh-in wanting to honor Ali. I must admit, I was enjoying pretending that I was Ali.

It was not only making me feel good but at the same time, by the role playing of Ali, was giving me confidence.

So, here I was, in my white satin robe and slippers walking down the hallways at Resorts Hotel heading to the showroom with my entourage of Dom, Tom, John, and Rich. I was shadow boxing at the same time that I kept chanting, "The champ is coming, the champ is coming."

When I entered the showroom, I shouted out, "The champ is here, the champ is here." At that moment, all the reporters that were interviewing the other fighters immediately left them and all flocked to me.

It was very easy to notice that the attention that I was receiving from the press was irritating all the other fighters on the card, especially the two fighters that were the main event.

The main subject that all the reporters wanted me to talk about was, how could you have such incredible punching power, especially being an old man?

I would give them answers that would make many of them laugh. Of course, I always used the spinach, Popeye, and pasta explanation. The new answer that I gave them for this fight was that I have disciplined myself to only have sexual intercourse five times per week.

I really enjoy making the press laugh kidding about my age. What I didn't do was disrespect my opponent or try to get laughs at the expense of my opponent.

I'm in the dressing room having my hands taped by Tommy and Luz, it was then that I began to meditate. As I was going into deep thought my consciousness was telling me to enjoy and savor the entire pageantry that I find myself in.

After the guys completed taping my hands, Tommy slapped my right hand which took me out of my deep thought.

When I lifted my fists and saw the great job that they had done, I said to them, "it looks like we're ready for Vegas."

A moment later, Dom comes over and says, "Put your robe on, we'll be going out in a minute."

As I took my first step into the entrance of the 19,000-seat arena, what I began to hear over the sound system throughout the building was the voice of Frank Sinatra singing my favorite song, "My Way."

At that moment I was reminded about the thought I had earlier of enjoying and savoring all the pageantry that I'm being part of.

As I continued walking down the steps toward the ring, the crowd started to notice that it was me.

Within a second the noise level was deafening. As I continued the walk toward the ring, I was looking in every direction as I was witnessing the reaction of the people.

By the time I entered the ring, the song had just ended. It was then that I stood in the middle of the ring and put my arms both high above my head, at that moment, the crowd began to chant, "Grandpa Doc, Grandpa Doc."

As I was gazing out into the crowd, I was becoming very emotional. As I continued to stand in the middle of the ring with my arms still high above my head, I started to see myself as a Roman gladiator preparing myself to face a three-day starved ferocious lion.

As I stared into the crowd, I was seeing a group of bloodthirsty Roman citizens sitting in the colosseum, anxiously waiting for the show to begin.

After meeting in the middle of the ring, the referee gave us the instructions. I then headed back to my corner waiting for the bell to ring.

That's when Luz asked the question, "How do you feel?" I answered his question by saying, "Start packing your bags for Vegas."

I gave Luz that response because I could feel this incredible superman strength slowly start entering my body as I started to walk toward the ring while I was hearing my song being played on the P.A. sound system.

That unexplainable strength continued to enter my body as I became more emotional as I looked into the crowd.

My last final thought that I had before the bell rang was what my opponent said to the press at the weigh-in, "I'm going to immediately come at the old man as soon as the bell rings with a barrage of left-right punches that will be impossible for him to block them all."

When the bell rang my opponent immediately ran toward me, by the time that he threw his first punch, I countered with a right cross that literally lifted this huge man off the ground before he went crashing to the canvas.

The crowd could not believe what their eyes had witnessed. The TV announcers were reacting in a manner, that despite the incredible volume of noise from the crowd, the announcers were still able to be heard up here in the ring.

They were saying even Mike Tyson never did it so fast.

Before the TV announcers and news reporters were able to make it up to the ring, I grabbed Dom and told him to get security to escort me to the dressing room immediately, "You, Tom and Luz do the interviews."

In a matter of seconds, there were four security guards helping me out of the ring. They then were draped around me as we were heading to the dressing room. While we were walking, the crowd started chanting throughout the arena, "Grandpa Doc, Grandpa Doc, Grandpa Doc."

When I entered the dressing room, to my surprise anxiously waiting for me was my daughter, Gina, and her mother, my ex-wife, Louise.

After we all hugged, I addressed a question to them both, "Ok, who gave me up?" "It had to be bucket mouth number one, Brian."

Gina replied, "Not really dad, Amy gave a little slip of the tongue to mommy, and then mommy opened Brian up like he was a walnut." We all then started laughing.

Gina then said, "This place was filled with celebrities, I even saw my idol from a distance, Sylvester Stallone. I still have a crush on him."

When I heard that I jumped up and got excited, as I said, "Do you think he's still around?" Gina replied, "Dad, he's long gone."

"Damn it, I wanted to try to get him to have dinner with us, I haven't forgotten that I promised you that."

After saying those words to my daughter, the entourage came marching into the dressing room. Luzzi was doing the cha-cha as he was singing, "Here we come Las Vegas, here we come!" Tommy and Richie were behind Luz as they were both singing, "Viva Las Vegas, Viva Las Vegas."

A minute later Dom came walking into the dressing room with my son, Brian, right behind his ass, bitching and moaning. Before the door closed four more bodies had entered the dressing room. They were Brian's three close friends,

Michael, Eddie, and Robin, my nephew, John, was also with them.

After my son hugged me and asked me if I was alright, he went back to his moaning. He was saying that security wasn't letting them into the dressing room; I kept saying that's my father in there. My mother and sister are also in there with him.

One of the security guards responded by saying, "I don't care if your grandmother is also in there, without a security pass you're not getting in." I was just getting ready to start yelling when Dom was walking toward the dressing room.

When Dom pulled up I said, "Dom, please tell these gentlemen who I am." Dom responded by saying, "He's the old man's son."

I then said to my son, everyone here is going right now to the Italian restaurant, I'm sure that will relax you, everyone started laughing.

Earlier today, I had Richie make dinner reservations for fifteen, I'm sure that there is not more than fifteen here.

Dom will wait with me till I take my shower and then we will meet all of you up there. Luzzi put his arm around Louise, and they led the crowd to the restaurant.

It had taken only a short time for me to shower and get dressed before Dom and I were headed to the restaurant.

When we arrived, Brian informed us that he already had the waiter take our orders. When I started to laugh, Louise said, "He acts like he never ate before." I replied, "I guess the apple doesn't fall far from the tree." Everyone started to laugh. I then said, "If you plant a potato, you can't expect to get a cucumber." Again, everyone began to laugh.

After dinner, but before we were served dessert, my son, nephew, and their friends, now that their bellies were full, were eager to get up off the table and rush to the casino for some action.

During the time that the rest of us were having our dessert, I asked my daughter, "When are you and your mom going to be leaving?"

Gina replied, "Daddy our flight leaves tomorrow morning at 9:00 a.m."

That's when Tommy asked Louise the question, "How are you getting to the AC airport?"

Louise's response was, "We're going to take a taxi."

Tommy then said, "My limo driver will be in front of the hotel tomorrow morning waiting for you and Gina to take you to the airport."

"Thanks Tom, that's very considerate of you," was Louise's comment.

I then said to Gina, "I want to have you and your husband my guests in Vegas for three days for the fight next month. Call your three brothers and invite them and their wives to also come as my guests."

Turning to Louise I said, "I want to invite you to come to the fight as my personal guest."

Before Louise could reply, Gina responded by saying, "Dad, mommy will accept only under one condition, you both have to have separate rooms."

I came back at my daughter's comment, "Gi, your mother is old enough to speak for herself." Everyone at the table started to laugh as Louise blushed.

After we all completed having our dessert, Gina told me that she was now going to take her mother to the casino to teach her how to throw the dice.

I responded, "Oh my God, the poor girl has my blood!" That's when Louise, as she was getting up from the table to follow her daughter, said, "Hey T, you plant a potato, you're going to get a potato." All the guys started laughing.

After Gina and Louise left, even though I knew that all the guys wanted to follow them to the casino, I told the guys that we had to stay at the table for a short meeting.

I then turned to Tommy and said, "I want my two brothers, John and Mark, to join our team." I then asked Tommy to find two positions in the Beyond the Beyond Corporation for them.

I also mentioned to Tom that I want them to become part of our entourage and come with us whenever it's about boxing or my public speaking.

Tommy became elated hearing the news. My brother, John, and Tom had become brothers ever since they started high school together and remained close friends for all these years.

There was one last thing that I asked of Tommy, and that was to inform John and Mark that they will be coming with us to Vegas for the fight.

I also told Tommy to have John bring his soulmate, Patty, with him. I also wanted Tommy to have Mark invite his ex-wife, Donna Marie, to come with us to Vegas.

I then turned to Richie and Dom and said, "I want you to invite your girlfriend and you, Dom, your ex-wife to Vegas as our guests.

The first to respond was Dom when he said, "Are you kidding me, you think this is going to be a picnic? I'm going to be so freaking busy out there as your representative, I won't have time for anything else. Just the Nevada State Boxing Commission will be breaking my balls over little bullshit things a day or two before the fight."

There's going to be media day, which both Rich and I will be busy with the entire day. Nobody but me realizes our present situation.

Dom then said to me, "You're going to be fighting the number ten ranked fighter in the world in Las Vegas on the undercard of the Middleweight Championship of the world. It's going to be televised on Pay-Per-View all over the world. Now, to put the cherry on the cake, next month you're going to be the hottest story in the country. A seventy-three-year-old man fighting a top-ranked professional boxer in Las Vegas is even better than Evel Knievel jumping the Caesar's Palace water fountains. Let me tell you guys another thing, the last few days till fight time, things are going to get really crazy, you will be amazed."

Dom then turned to me and said, "Thank God you put your two brothers onto our team because we're certainly going to need them."

Dom continued on, "Now if you win this fight, FORGET ABOUT IT, things will become uncontrollable. I don't know if any of you really understand that this fight in Vegas will be worldwide."

"Oh my God," was Richie's reaction when he heard that, he then said, "I'm Doc's PR man, I could see the job that's ahead of me."

Dom then said, "Wait until you see the celebrities that will be there. All your top movie stars and famous people will be crawling all around Caesar's Palace that entire weekend."

Hearing that, I became excited and said, "Oh Wow!" "Maybe my sweetheart, Jennifer Aniston will be there. I have such a crush on her, I really love her, I find her to be so adorable."

"Son of a bitch," was Dom's reaction after hearing my comment. He said to the guys, "You see what I'm up against; he'll get excited over Jennifer Aniston, but not the fight."

Rich then said, "Doc, I would have turned down the offer to bring the girl I date to Vegas anyway in hopes that I might meet many girls out there. But now after hearing what Dom had to say, I probably will not have the time to play around anyway."

There is one last issue Rich, that I would like to go over with you. Any speaking engagements that you can arrange between now and when we go to Vegas will be fine.

Once we go to Vegas, and as long as I keep winning, I will not do any public speaking. I will only resume my public speaking if I lose a fight or win the championship.

Just like we all expected, the next morning I was all over the newspapers in Philly, Jersey, and New York along with all their local TV news channels. Even the local talk shows were talking about me.

As we were all having our breakfast in the living room of one of our suites before leaving A.C. to head back home, Tom and John were reading all the different stories in the tri-state newspapers.

That's when Dom said to all of us, "fellas you see all the publicity that Doc is receiving here in this tri-state area, just imagine every major newspaper in every major city in the country, not to even mention every national TV news channel."

"I'm not even bringing up all the countries of the world that will be writing and talking about Doc, so do you all see my point on the importance of this Vegas fight?"

As soon as we arrived back up north, I told the guys that I'm immediately going incognito. I will only see you guys each day for my workouts, or if I have a speaking engagement, which will all be predicated on Rich.

I intend to spend the next three and one-half weeks before we head to Vegas on meditating and doing my writing. My recreation will be spending some time with my grandkids when they have time for me.

The way things turned out; Rich had not scheduled any speaking engagements for me during this time. I must say that my premonition is telling me that Dom, and possibly all the guys had something to do with that.

My thinking is that Dom discouraged Rich from setting up any speaking engagements for me knowing that I would put all my attention concentrating on my speaking rather than on the upcoming fight.

Three and a half weeks went by lightning-fast and before I even realized, our expanded entourage of my two brothers, John and Mark, were boarding a TWA aircraft that was headed, non-stop to the eighth wonder of the world.

As we were circling Vegas, we started slowly descending before landing, at that moment, it was impossible to not notice the tremendous lighting of the Las Vegas strip.

The glamour and glitz of the city made it difficult for anyone not to get excited knowing where they were. This truly is an oasis that was placed in the middle of the desert.

After we landed, Caesar's had two stretch limos waiting for our entourage.

When we all checked in, we were placed into two of the topmost luxurious four-bedroom penthouses in the hotel. I decided that we would pair off into three and four, I had Tom, Luz, Rich, and Dom put into the one suite and then the three brothers into the second suite.

After we all unpacked and got settled in, we all went to the hotel's boxing gym. Wow! We were all impressed with what modern-day technology has done for sports training.

There were so many different pieces of scientific equipment that were designed specifically for the modern-day boxer.

As advantageous as all this modern-day apparatus could be for a fighter, I told Dom that in the next few days up to the fight, I'm not going to use any of it.

I told Dom the reason was because I would be using my muscles in a different way and it's too late to use that equipment for this fight.

I then made a commitment to Dom that if I ever win the championship, I will have a modern-day boxing gym built with all the modern-day machines and technology, and I will put it in his name as a gift.

The only commitment that I asked of Dom was that he name the gym Curly and Dom's Modern-Day Boxing Gym in honor of my father.

After touring the gym everyone was eager to go outside and walk the famous walkway that takes you to the back of the hotel, where there sits the famous 20,000 seat outdoor arena.

Just like the two great middleweights that will be getting into the ring Saturday night, this arena has hosted many other great middleweights that now have become legends.

Sugar Ray Leonard, Roberto Duran, Thomas Hearns, Marvin Hagler, and Manny Pacquiao, just to mention a few of the greats who have stepped into this ring.

I believe that when we all observed that famous outdoor arena, we all started to really see the magnitude of the event that we were all about to take part in.

Now that we went through some of the famous boxing nostalgia of Caesar's Palace, we all went to eat at the hotel's famous Italian restaurant.

After dinner, all the guys decided to walk around the casino and the hotel. Every one of the guys was enjoying all the pageantry and the flood of all the celebrities coming into town for the big fight night.

I believe that I decided to stay in seclusion because I was starting to feel the pressure of how really big this opportunity was going to be. I also started to realize that now I was going to be fighting one of the best in the world, and if I lost, all this pageantry and excitement would be over. At the same time, I was also trying to stay focused; all of what I'm doing at this time is secondary to what my true mission and purpose are. Just like life in general, you blink your eyes and a few days have passed by, you start to daydream and weeks or possibly months could have flown by. I say this because I opened my eyes and saw that it was only a few hours before fight time. It turned out that everyone that I invited, my four children and their spouses, my kid's mom, and all the guys' wives or soulmates showed up and stopped by to wish me luck.

As Tommy and Luzzi were taping my hands, Tommy excitedly said, "Guess who I ran into a few hours ago in the casino, LT, Lawrence Taylor. I was telling him how you had invited me and a few other friends to his grand opening of his night club, LT's."

Doc, would you believe that Lawrence remembered the incident that you told us about when LT's golf partner from Florida said something that you didn't like, and how LT immediately went over to him and advised him to come over to you and apologize.

That's when Luzzi interjected when he said, "Doc, that story is in your first book."

Tommy's response was, "Yeah Luz, you're right." Tom then said, "LT told me the same story as you told us many years ago."

During the rest of the time that it took to complete taping my hands, and then after, I didn't have much, if anything to say. I completely went into a meditative state.

I only came out of my meditation when Dom walked into the dressing room and said, "Doc, put your robe on, it's fight time."

It was only then that I started to question if I would receive the super-strength that would be necessary to win the fight.

As I began to enter the arena they started to play, "My Way," by Frank Sinatra. Surprisingly to me, the crowd's reaction after seeing me walking toward the ring wasn't as great as the last fight that I had in Atlantic City.

Just like Dom said, I haven't been getting the publicity that I have been getting on the east coast anywhere else. As I continued walking toward the ring, it then came to me what Dom said, "This is my opportunity to have the world know of me."

As I was climbing up the steps to enter the ring, I was totally focused on what was at hand. I knew that I was going to have to stay focused so that I could try and stir my emotions in a way that the super-strength will enter my body.

After I entered the ring, Dom, Tom, and Luz followed. It was then that Luzzi mentioned to me, "Wow, Jennifer Aniston is sitting right here in the first row, she looks really hot in that white dress all tanned up."

When I heard that, I became so excited that it was hard to control. I kept trying to look where she was sitting and trying not to have it look obvious.

I then started to become out of control talking really fast to Luzzi. I was saying, "I love that girl, I have a crush on her, I find her to be adorable."

When Dom started to see that I was losing focus on the fight that was shortly about to start, he began yelling at Luzzi,

"Why did you tell this crazy man what you saw?" Dom then started to yell at me, "you crazy fuck, come down and sit on the stool."

Dom then started to put Vaseline on my face as he was rubbing my neck. I guess that he was trying to relax me. I then started to yell at Dom when his hand went across my head, I said, "Dom, what the hell are you doing, you're messing my hair."

That's when Dom really went nuts as he said, "What hair are you talking about, the two hairs that you have on each side of your head, you crazy person?"

At that moment I got up off the stool and pretended that I was warming up, but in reality, I was only trying to get to the side of the ring where Jennifer was sitting.

I then started to wonder if she was going to root for me, I would be heartbroken if she was going to root against me.

It was time to go to the center of the ring for instructions from the referee. Words cannot express how intimidating my opponent appeared, many would say that he looked frightening.

The funny thing is that I didn't even pay attention to his appearance or let it be intimidating to me; all I had on my mind was that Jennifer Aniston was looking at me at that very moment.

When the bell rang, I tried to show off by dancing around the ring like when I was young. Dom seeing that knew it was a big mistake because he knew I only had a certain amount of energy to spare.

So, Dom started to yell to me, "Doc, stop dancing," but I didn't listen to him; I kept trying to show-off with some of the footwork that I use to have many, many years ago.

It was at that moment when I was on the side of the ring where Jennifer was sitting, that I tried to get a glance at her, it was then that I didn't see the right cross that was coming toward me.

The punch landed square on my jaw and I went down to one knee. Even though my head was not clear, I still tried to see if Jennifer was rooting for me.

It was only after I heard the referee count to nine that I immediately jumped up. I began to go back to dancing, but within seconds the bell rang.

When I returned to the corner Dom was going crazy, he was yelling, "What are you doing?" You're going to blow everything."

As I started to throw water on my head, I began to yell at him to stop messing up my hair. It was then that I turned to Luzzi and said, "Luz, is Jennifer rooting for me?" "Was she happy to see me knocked down?"

Luz answered, "This bitch was laughing and making fun of you. She was happy that you got knocked down and she wants to see you get knocked out, she's a real bitch."

Hearing what Luzzi told me, it was difficult to remain on the stool to wait for the bell to ring. When the bell finally rang, I came out so infuriated, when I was about to throw my punch, it's like a small earthquake was about to take place when I let go, half the desert shook when my opponent went flying over the ropes and went crashing onto the TV announcers table.

It was then when I looked into the crowd with a mean and stern look that I saw Jennifer jumping up and down with joy. She had a big smile on her face, as I looked into her eyes, she winked at me.

After now knowing that she was rooting for me, I leaned over the ropes and said, "I have a crush on you, I find you to be adorable." It was then that she threw me a kiss.

During the time that I was on the ropes communicating with Jennifer, my entire entourage came into the ring. Along with Dom, Tom and Luz were my two brothers, John and Mark, plus Richie. Those three came into the ring wearing red baseball jackets with white lettering saying, Grandpa Doc Staff.

Those six bodies would not allow anyone, including the TV announcer to get to me until I finished with Jennifer.

When the TV announcer from the Pay-Per-View came to me, he was going nuts, he couldn't believe what he saw, even though he had heard stories about my other fights.

Another announcer came over and he was so excited that he was stuttering when he said, "No one has ever seen anyone with the punching power to actually lift a 230-pound fighter, in real life, off his feet and up into the air and over the ropes. Then to think that it's coming from a man of your age, it's more than incredible."

My response was the same as my other fights, "I eat my spinach like Popeye, but not out of the can. I eat my spinach sautéed with olive oil and garlic over a bed of pasta." I then let Dom handle the interview. I immediately grabbed Luzzi and said, "You bastard, you lied to me, Jennifer Aniston was rooting for me." Luzzi's response was, "Doc, that was the only chance that we had to win the fight. I had to lie to get you mad enough to take your anger out on your opponent."

Luz added, "It was also the only chance that I had to reprieve myself, you do remember that I was the one that made the mistake to tell you that Jennifer Aniston was at the fight."

So, the way that I'm seeing it, everyone is going to believe that the reason why I won was that I became so angry thinking that Jennifer Aniston was rooting against me.

Truth be told, that thought alone would not have done it, but it is true that it was my anger that was able to ignite and stir my emotions to a point that allowed the super-strength to enter my body.

Of course, I can't allow anyone to know my secret, so it's good that everyone believes it was solely my anger that was responsible for any success.

Chapter Eleven

After I took my shower and got dressed, our entire entourage went back to our suite. Win or lose, Dom had made arrangements to have the hotel caterer set up the living room of our suite with the finest hors-d'oeuvres.

Knowing that all our loved ones were going to be coming in shortly, I grabbed Dom, Tom, and Luz and said, "Please don't break my balls about Jennifer Aniston in front of everyone, keep it our secret."

Just bringing that situation up, got Dom all worked up all over again. He started saying to my brothers, John and Mark, "Your sick brother was complaining that I was messing his hair during the fight," all the guys started laughing.

Dom then said, I guess he meant the two hairs that he has on each side of his head, everyone now was laughing hysterically.

At that moment, Tommy's wife, Bernadette, Luzzi's wife, Maryann, brother John's soulmate, Patty, brother Mark's and my ex-wives, Donna Marie and Louise, all came walking into the suite to celebrate.

It seemed like only a few minutes had passed by when my four kids came walking in with their spouses.

Everyone was laughing, telling jokes, celebrating and having a good time. Most everyone there was talking and bragging about how many celebrities that they saw.

That's when my son, Brian, said, "Whatcha talking about, I helped Jennifer Aniston walk down the stairs in her high heels to the VIP section, she looked hot."

Luzzi tried to hold back his laughter, but it shortly turned into choking, from the shrimp that he was eating. That's when I went over to him and slapped him so hard on the back the shrimp came shooting out of his mouth like a bullet.

I then said, "My dear friend, you should not be laughing while you're eating."

We all partied into the night till the wee hours of the morning, despite everyone having a flight scheduled to go back home later that day.

It was only our entourage that would be staying an extra two days because we had a very important meeting scheduled with the executives of Caesar's Boxing Promotions.

The way the meeting turned out was that Caesar's Boxing Promotion was becoming a co-promoter along with Madison Square Garden. They offered me a deal to fight the former heavyweight champion for a guaranteed purse of five million dollars.

Along with that, there was a stipulation that if I win that fight, I would be guaranteed a fight for the heavyweight championship of the world.

If that happens, I would have still had one more pro fight than Leon Spinks when he fought Mohammad Ali for the heavyweight championship after only having seven pro fights.

All the guys advised me that I could get more than five million. They said that I had become not only the hottest fighter in boxing but also the hottest thing in all sports. Of course, the biggest reason for that was my age.

My answer to them was, "It's better than two million that we received for last night's fight."

That's when Dom said, once they started having all the big fights on Pay-Per-View, the fighters purses all started to sky-rocket.

One of the most important things to me about this upcoming fight is that it will be held in Madison Square Garden. All the nostalgia that this place holds means very much to me.

I then said to Tommy, once the two million dollar check is deposited into the Beyond the Beyond Corporation and it clears, I want you to buy a new Mercedes for each of the guys that are part of the entourage. That would be you, Luzzi, Richie, Dom, John and Mark.

Tommy's response was, "What about you?"

My response was, "I don't need one." I then told Tommy to order an extra stretch limo for our entourage.

Tommy then asked, "Is that it?"

"Not quite," was my response. "I want you to order three more Mercedes, one for each of the three loves of my life, Louise, Angie, and Marie."

I then said to Tommy, "all the rest of the money that I make through boxing will be donated to the Beyond the Beyond Corporation for our entourage expenses along with cost and distribution of all my books to be sent around the world."

I then said to all the guys, we're only two fights away from completing our goals. I will then be able to go on my final journey to complete my DESTINY.

After Dom heard my comment he replied, "I can't believe what I have witnessed, not only did we win the fight, but we're going home knowing that we have one of the biggest fights that you could ever imagine already arranged."

Dom continued on by saying to all of us, "I didn't even mention to you guys but the only reason we had this opportunity for this fight was because the number one ranked heavyweight had to cancel six weeks before the fight."

Dom then looked at me and said, "Just maybe there is something to why you keep saying DESTINY."

Tommy then said to us, "Fellas, this is how we're all getting new cars, the first fight was for $2,000, the second fight was for $5,000. The next four fights were for $10,000, $20,000, $40,000, and then $80,000."

Last night's fight was for two million and in six weeks that fight will be for five million.

That's when Luzzi jumped into the conversation by saying, "You win the next fight, and I'll bet anyone that you will get $100 million for the championship fight."

Dom immediately responded to Luzzi's statement, "you are not wrong, just two years ago, Connor McGregor, the kick-boxer champ received 100 million for fighting Floyd Mayweather Jr."

Floyd actually made even more than 100 million, and it wasn't even a heavyweight championship fight.

He then added, "you see what I mean when I say that the Pay-Per-View is what sky-rocketed the fighter's purses for big fights."

Hearing those numbers started to get me a little wound up, even though money has never been a motivating factor for me to be inspired to reach my goals.

I then called Rich over and asked him if he would call the airlines and cancel my flight back to Newark Airport with you guys. I would like you then to please get me a flight to West Palm Beach Airport; hopefully you will be able to get me on the same flight as my brother, John.

I told my brother, John, that I'm going back to Florida with him, hopefully on the same flight. I let him know that I have to go visit Mother and Daddy's grave. I told him that I'll stay with him for the night and then go back to Jersey the following day.

After Richie got off the phone, he brought me the good news that I'll be going on the same flight as my brother to Florida.

My brother, Mark, was unable to make the trip with me to our parents' gravesite because he had a previous commitment that he needed to attend to in Jersey.

As John and I were on the plane, I started to laugh, I then said to him, "I could just feel Daddy's spirit, I know he is really enjoying all of this, just knowing how much he loved the sport of boxing."

"John, most important, I need to speak to our Mother's spirit at her resting place tomorrow." That's when my brother said, tomorrow morning after we have breakfast, you're going to take my car and drive me to Patty's house; then you could go to the cemetery and spend as much time as you like.

John then said, "I don't need to go with you, I stop by the grave for a few minutes every week, my home is ten minutes from the cemetery."

John continued on, "I'm sure after spending time at the gravesite; you're going to want to go around the corner to where Mother and Daddy's condo was."

"I'm sure you're going to want to reflect on all the great and sad times that we had at that place as a family."

I was emotional, but I still started to laugh, as I said to my brother, "Wow!" "You're right, that's exactly what I'm going to be doing."

I then decided to tease my brother a little, when I said, "I can't believe you're not giving me instructions on how to be careful driving your car."

My brother has been known for literally rubbing the paint off his cars from cleaning them so often.

"Oh, shit John, it just came to me, I found the answer, you're not worried about me driving your car knowing that you're going to be getting a new Mercedes." We both started laughing.

As I was walking toward the grave site, when I began to get close, the tears began to flow. Shortly after standing by their gravestone, I began to reminisce about the times I heard my mother's spirit speak to me.

I then thanked her for all the signs that she has given me, that proved to me without any doubt, from all the worldly evidence that she provided to me, to show that I truly heard her voice speak to me.

Now it was time for me to speak to her. I told her that I remember the last words that she said to me before her spirit left her physical body for her journey to the Beyond the Beyond.

Those words were, love the Lord Jesus and his blessed mother with all your heart. I have always tried my best to adhere to those words.

Standing by the gravestone as I was looking at my mom's name, I gave thanks to my mother's spirit for giving me the inspiration that I needed to complete my goals so I could then go on my mission to spread the message that I received from my mother's spirit.

I then let her know that I honor my Lord and Savior, Jesus Christ, for allowing my mother's spirit to watch over me.

I said to my Dad, tell everyone in heaven to root for me, I have two more fights to go before I complete my goal, but most important, I pray that I will not allow myself to hurt anyone.

I said to my mother, "Ma, I'm getting ready to fulfill my purpose in life by spreading your message from Beyond the Beyond," I then kissed their stone, and told them that I loved them.

It was then that it happened, as I started to get emotional, I felt this sudden burst of super-strength entering my body, but like never before. This time it just kept pouring into me like an electric current would go through a wire.

Becoming concerned about what I was experiencing, I kept trying to tell myself to relax and calm down; hopefully this power will stop entering my body.

After I decided to walk to the car, I was now going to be headed to where my Mom and Dad's retirement village was. It was only a half-mile from the cemetery, right off of Federal Highway.

Right alongside the cemetery was Federal Highway. After getting on that road, it was no more than a quarter of a mile up the road that I saw a car completely in flames.

There had to be at least five cars parked alongside the burning vehicle. There was a large group of people all around the car, but they were all helpless as they watched a young man and woman being burnt to death.

I stopped my brother's car in the middle of the highway, got out, and ran to the burning car, when I got there, it was hard to see if they were still alive.

I took my shirt off, wrapped it around my hands and ripped the door right off the car. As I was running to the other side of the car, I was yelling at the people to drag the driver out of the car.

After ripping the door on the other side of the car right off, I dragged the young woman out of the burning car. All the people that were around the car, helpless were now trying to help the young man and woman.

When I started to run to my brother's car, I heard the sound of sirens coming from a distance. All the people there were so pre-occupied with administering to the victims that they didn't even realize with all the excitement and commotion that I took off.

I had become very nervous that I might get discovered because I knew that no man could have been able to literally rip two car doors right off a car with their bare hands like they were superman.

I was no longer going to go to the retirement village; it was too close to where the accident occurred. So, what I did was drive directly to my brother's house and I stayed there.

I called John at Patty's house and told him that I can't pick him up, I told him to have Patty take him home. I wasn't sure if any of the people got John's license plate number or a description of his car.

I was really happy that my flight was for 9:00 a.m. tomorrow, I wanted to get out of town as fast as I can.

Sure enough, the event that occurred today was on the evening news and not in a small way. Witnesses were claiming that it was an old man that jumped out of his car that appeared to be a pearl colored Cadillac; he ran to the scene and ripped both doors off the burning car with his bare hands.

The news said that although the two victims have life-threatening burns, doctors feel there is a good chance they are going to survive.

That evening three different news channels were interviewing different eyewitnesses that were at the scene of the burning car and the incredible unexplainable rescue that took place earlier today.

The good part of what I was hearing from the different eyewitnesses was that they all were so nervous and taken back from the horrific event before their eyes, everyone was giving different descriptions of me.

The only consensus of all the eyewitnesses was that it was an old man that did the impossible.

During the viewing of the TV news that occurred earlier today, John had already arrived back home from Patty's, but thank God, he was preoccupied doing something in the other part of the house.

The next morning, I was up early, and John was driving me to the airport. As he was dropping me off, I told him that Tommy would be calling him about when to fly up to Jersey now that he's part of the entourage.

When I entered the airport, the first thing I did was to go to the newsstand and buy many of the different newspapers.

All the papers that I bought had extensive stories about the burning car and how unexplainably and miraculously two people were saved when this allegedly old man came on the scene and became superman-like by ripping both doors off the burning car with his bare hands.

After arriving back in Jersey, the first thing I did was buy all the big New York and New Jersey newspapers. I was really hoping they didn't cover the Florida story.

It turned out that I wasn't so lucky; in fact, all these papers were really making a big story out of this Florida accident.

They're now trying to tie this mysterious Florida story to the Jersey mysterious story; how allegedly, a superman-like old man came onto the scene and took an overturned truck, picked it up, and put it right side up to save the driver's life.

It turned out I did get lucky with the guys in our entourage. Being that the guys have been so busy in their personal lives lately with all the excitement and acknowledgements that they have been getting, they had no time to be looking at the news on TV.

Because of the guys being so involved and part of our quest to capture the heavyweight championship of the world, they haven't even had time to pick up the paper.

I did have a concern that if the guys started to put all the pieces of the puzzle together from both stories, it would be hard for me to explain.

Later that day, I called each one of the guys separately to let them know that we will all go back to work tomorrow. I did inform each one that we will be having a meeting in Dom's office before I start my workout.

When speaking with Rich, I asked him if he would work on purchasing a two-bedroom condo for me. I told him that it has to be in my immediate area of North Arlington, Lyndhurst, Rutherford, Nutley, or Clifton.

Rich replied, "I'll start working on that immediately. As your P.R. man, there is not much to do. Lately ever since Vegas, you have become world-known."

I started to laugh before I said to Rich, "two more fights and we will have reached our goals, it is then that we start our mission."

The next day when we arrived at the gym, we were all surprised to see a fairly large group of fans waiting in the front of the gym for me. Many were taking pictures, and some were asking for autographs.

When we began to enter the gym, there stood this huge muscular man, he was allowing the news media, but no fans could enter the gym.

After entering the gym, there sat a group of reporters sitting in the grandstands at the sparring area, waiting for my arrival.

When we saw this, we immediately started to walk really fast into Dom's office where Dom was sitting behind his desk waiting for us.

After we all sat down, Dom said, "I'll start the meeting. If you're all ready, I told all of you if we win this fight in Vegas, everything is going to instantaneously change for all of us."

"If we win the next two fights, it will be the greatest achievement in the history of boxing; it will be the greatest feat in the history of all sports."

"You guys may be asking, why is Dom always saying WE, when it would have been Doc's achievement?" "I'm telling all of you that we're a team. I'm telling all of you that if WE win the next two fights, Johnny Luzzi, who forgot to bring the stool up into the ring when the bell rang, has the chance to go down in history along with Tommy and myself, as one of the great fight trainers."

I spoke next, when I said to Tommy, "Tom, before I ask Luzzi for his autograph, I need you to call my brother, Mark and have him become part of our entourage. Have your driver start picking Mark up along with us whenever we go anywhere."

Tom, I need you to immediately take your driver off your payroll and put him on the Beyond the Beyond Corporation's payroll. I want you to also go back as far as it was that we started using him, and I want you to be reimbursed for his pay.

Tom, I also need you to purchase one more Mercedes for Kim, that's Ronnie Kist's wife. She does all my secretarial work for all of my books.

That's when Tommy said, "Why don't you have her become our secretary?" My response was, "No way Tom, will we hire a secretary. Kim very special, only she is allowed to be part of my writing."

"If I win this next fight and get the chance for the title, win or lose, I'm having you write her a check for five million for believing in me."

I now informed the guys that I'm immediately going into seclusion for the next five and a half weeks.

"Only if it's mandatory that Caesar's Palace-Madison Square Garden Co-Promotion has me do a press conference, you guys will be responsible for everything, including all media interviews."

"I'm hoping that during this time before the fight, I become inspired to continue my writing. I'm also hoping that by listening to my music during this time I will be given the insight to find the words to write a song."

"There is one last thing that I would like to express to you guys, and that is the honor that I feel to be fighting in Madison Square Garden, this is very special to me."

I then asked the guys if they had any questions. When no one answered, Dom said in an authoritative voice, "Ok Doc, go put your workout clothes on, Tom and John, start to tape his hands, Rich go talk to the news reporters. They're all around the sparring area."

After only a few days in seclusion, I decided to go meditate in the church that I grew up in. It's been quite some time since I have last been in that church.

I have so many special memories of the church. The one that always brings tears to my eyes is when my mother told me that my father began to cry when he saw me go up to receive Communion.

For some reason that has always touched my heart, to think that my father would become so emotional watching his young, skinny son with these very thick coke bottle eyeglasses go up to the altar to profess his faith.

I then started to laugh when I began to reflect back to being a kid with my older brother, John. Sometimes we would skip going to church so that we could hang on the corner with our friends.

So, what my mother would do is give us a test when we came home. We would have to tell her what color the priest's vestments were at mass. We would also have to tell her what the sermon was for that day's mass.

Sometimes we would guess right. When we guessed wrong, we would get punished.

As I sat in the pew, I gave thanks for all the good that was given to me throughout my life. I acknowledged all the mistakes that I had made. I accepted the deep sorrow that harbors within my heart for the wrong that I have done.

I have tremendous gratitude that I was given the opportunity, despite my sins, to bring some good into the world.

Most of all, I am humbled, sometimes even confused, why me, that I have seen the so many signs that were given to me throughout my life. To know that I have experienced most of all the good and bad that this world could bring.

Now, in the twilight of my life, I see why I was given the power to hear my mother's spirit speak to me. I see why I chose the road of life that I had taken, and now I will bring forth my final purpose in life, the message from Beyond the Beyond.

Before I left the church, I acknowledged that I was not delusional or blinded by what I have achieved in the ring. I am fully in touch with reality and the fact that only through this special strength that enters my body, am I capable of achieving my goals.

Knowing that I have already achieved what I set out to accomplish, being well known enough for people to come out and hear my word, this goal has already been fulfilled.

For this reason, I have no insight if I will be successful in this upcoming fight.

Getting up off the bench as I started to leave the church, I repeated my mother's words that she said to me before she left this world, "Paulie, love the Lord Jesus and his blessed Mother with all of your heart."

Being into my family, meditating, and my writing, one day I woke up and became aware that it was one day before fight time.

Chapter Twelve

Today was the first day that I really paid attention to the fight that was before me. In fact, I really didn't pay any attention to what the guys were doing over these five weeks, even though I saw them for a few hours every day for my workouts.

I didn't ask and they didn't tell. I guess they kept the work that they were doing away from me, not to break my concentration on the fight. The funny thing was that the fight was the furthest thing from my mind.

I was truly touched when I became aware that Tommy, Luzzi, and Richie, along with their normal assignments for the cause, have been going out using their business and sales ability to get large companies to donate to our prison program.

They had even brought my brother, Mark, into the mix, and the same with my brother, John, in Florida.

Today is going to be the first press conference that I will be attending for this fight. I would have preferred not to be there, but it was in the contract that I be present.

This will be the first time that I will be face to face with Basso Bear, the former heavyweight champ. I do have much respect for the man, both as a fighter and as a person.

I was truly shocked when he lost his title by literally being demolished from the current champ, Jamel Perry. Before that fight he looked unbeatable, in fact, that fight with the present champ reminded me of the George Forman-Ken Norton fight with Basso being Ken Norton.

As we were driving over to Madison Square Garden for the press conference, I found myself starting to get a little nervous. Perhaps the reason was that I found myself unsure what I was going to say.

When we pulled up to that famous magnificent structure that took up the space of one city block in the greatest city in the world, seeing my name in bright lights on the marquee was like a fantasy.

Just like every other fight, the news media had a greater interest in me than my opponent. Since I was now fighting the former heavyweight champ, the interest in me was even greater.

I need not have to say, but from my first fight up until this fight, the great interest in me is all because of my age.

When the reporters asked me if I trained harder for this fight, knowing that my opponent was the former heavyweight champ, and by winning this fight, I would be getting a shot at the title, my answer was, "If I trained any harder or longer than I did at my age, I would be breaking down my body. If a man of my age trained harder than I did, he would be going in the opposite direction."

When the reporters asked me what my game plan was, did I have a strategy? I told them, honestly, I haven't even decided yet what pasta I'm going to be eating with my sautéed spinach for my pre-meal. Will it be spaghetti, linguine, or angel hair?

When the reporters asked Basso, what was his strategy, knowing that you will be fighting someone who hits as hard as the old man?

Basso's response was, "I will be taking advantage of my height, reach, speed, and youth. All his other opponents weren't patient; they didn't try to get him tired before they went to take him out."

When I heard Basso's comments, I was really concerned although I didn't try to show it. I was saying to myself; this guy is a complete double of Mohammad Ali in every which way.

This guy could dance and pick me apart with his long reach and his stiff jab. If he doesn't choose to mix it up, I'm in deep trouble. I'll never be able to get to him.

Once the press conference was completed, I became very frustrated after hearing my opponent speak about his fight strategy. Not wanting to concern Dom or the guys, I kept my frustrations to myself.

Knowing how to remedy that frustration, I told all the guys that since we're already in New York City, I want to go to Katz's Jewish Deli, it's the best in the country.

When we arrived at the Deli, just like always, day or night, it doesn't matter, there is always a long line to get into the joint.

So when our limo pulled up to the front door, it meant nothing, limos are going there all the time.

It was then that we got lucky, the guy at the door recognized me, so we didn't have to wait.

After we were seated, my brother, John noticed all the many pictures of celebrities on the walls, that's when he said to Dom, do you have a glossy of Doc in the limo? Dom's response was, "You have to ask Richie, he's the public relations man."

When Richie heard John's request, he ran out to the limo, under the seat was a draw, there was a folder with many glossy pictures of me. When Richie came back into the Deli, he had me sign the picture and then he gave it to the manager.

When I thought of the hundreds of big-time celebrities that were on that wall, which went back all the way to the thirties, I then began to realize what an honor it is for my picture to hang on one of those walls.

As good as the feeling was to have my picture be put onto the Katz's famous wall, the feeling was even better when I took a bite into a six inch high corn beef and pastrami that was laid upon the greatest rye bread that could be baked.

Their famous kosher pickles and coleslaw was like putting the icing on the cake. One thing for sure, having that corned beef and pastrami melt in my mouth surely took away the concern that I had for my opponent's strategy.

The next day at 5:00 p.m., our entourage was driving through the Lincoln Tunnel en route to the Garden. Dom wanted us to get there a little early, so we didn't have to rush later.

I didn't have a problem with that; I wanted to savor every moment of this monumental day. As our entourage slowly walked through the hallways to get to the dressing room, TV cameras followed us all the way.

That gave me a flashback to when I saw Mohammad Ali on television entering the Garden as the TV cameras followed him to the dressing room before his monumental first fight with Smoking Joe Frazier.

That fight went down in history as the greatest fight of the century.

At the Garden, one of the many good things is that they have excellent dressing rooms for the marquee fighters. They actually have a small parlor with couches and a TV.

Along with that, there is a refrigerator, microwave, and a table.

Having these conveniences was helpful to both myself and my entourage, knowing that we would be in that dressing room for many hours, up until fight time, which could be anywhere from 10:30 to 10:45 p.m.

About an hour before the fight, Dom had Tommy and Luzzi tape my hands. At that time, all fighters would start to warm up, but Dom knew that was not for me.

If I would have started to warm up an hour before the fight, I would have been too tired to get into the ring.

When an official from the New York State Boxing Commission walked into my dressing room and said to Dom, "Five minutes before show time." That was when I started to warm-up.

When Dom said to me, "Ok, put your robe on and let's go. That is when I said to myself, *I'm going to savor every moment of this event.*

Turning to Luzzi, I whispered, "Luz, look to see if Sandra Bullock is here, I really love her too." Luzzi's response was, "You're not getting me into trouble with Dom, concentrate on the fight, you crazy person."

I then turned to my brother, John, and asked him to put my eyeglasses on me. I'm sure that I was going to be the first boxer ever to be walking into the ring wearing eyeglasses, but I didn't care. I wanted to be able to clearly see everything.

As I began to enter the arena the fans started to erupt, as I continued to get closer to the ring the roar became deafening. Once I climbed the steps to enter the ring, that's when by wearing my eyeglasses, I was able to clearly see all the celebrities sitting by ringside.

The few that had gotten my attention, perhaps because they are some of my favorites were Robert DeNiro, Al Pacino, Martin Scorsese, Tom Hanks, and Clint Eastwood.

As I continued to look around ringside in hopes that I would see one of my sweethearts, Jennifer Aniston, or Sandra Bullock, Basso Bear entered the ring.

The former champ immediately got my attention the way he began to dance and prance around the ring. The way he moved and started to shadow box with lightning speed made me think that I was looking at Ali.

When we went to the center of the ring for our instructions from the referee, Basso towered over me being 6-3 versus my 5-10. When I was young, I was five foot eleven inches tall, but it is true what they say, when you get to old age, you start to shrink.

After I observed the tremendous reach of Basso as his arms hung alongside him during the ref's instructions, I knew that I was in big trouble.

When the bell rang, unfortunately I was right, Basso came out standing tall on his toes. He then began to stick that long arm out, as his fist went crashing into my face.

The problem that I feared is at hand. As he's throwing that stiff jab into my face, before I could even counter with a punch, his speed has him moving away.

When the bell rang to end round one, as I was returning to my corner, I was hoping that Dom had a solution for my problem. The first thing that Dom said was to Luzzi, he asked him for the metal plate that was in the ice bucket.

He then told Tommy, to hold the metal plate onto my badly swollen right eye. Dom then said to me, "Your right eye is closed, you won't be able to see out of that eye," I then told Tom, "It doesn't matter, I'm almost blind in that eye anyway."

Dom's solution to my problem was, "Doc, you have to pressure him, and try to get him against the ropes or into the corner." Before I could respond to Dom, the bell rang for round two.

When I went out to the center of the ring, I was rudely greeted with a really hard stiff jab, I must say, it really hurt. At least I thought it hurt until Basso showed me what a left, right combination felt like.

Along with the pain being excruciating, those punches were good enough to knock me down to one knee. While still being on the canvas, I could feel the blood streaming down the side of my face from a bad cut over my left eye.

When I came up onto my two feet, the count was at eight. I was very angry when I got up and I started to chase Basso all around the ring. I was trying my very best to hit him, but he was just too fast.

Then just when I got lucky and trapped Basso into the corner, the bell rang to end round two. As soon as I arrived at my corner, Dom immediately put a coagulant substance on my cut, he then put a piece of gauze over the cut and then told Tommy to hold the gauze on the cut and put pressure on it.

Luzzi then said, "Doc, do you want us to stop the fight," when I didn't answer, Tommy asked Dom, should we stop it? That's when Dom said to me, "Doc, I'm going to stop the fight, he's too fast, you have no chance against him, why should you get seriously hurt for no reason, plus your good eye is badly cut."

My response to Dom and all the guys was, "DESTINY if I don't win this fight, I will never get the opportunity to speak to 100,000 people in Giant Stadium."

At that moment, I became very emotional over the thought that my insight and premonition for speaking at Giant Stadium may never become a reality.

I then said to Dom, Tom, and Luz, "We could influence our destiny through our efforts and actions, give me one more round."

Before anyone could say another word, the bell rang for round three.

I can't even begin to express the feeling and emotions that I was experiencing at that moment. All I could remember as I got off the stool and went toward Basso was nothing will stop me from fulfilling my destiny.

At that instant, with some of the super-strength that had entered my body, I was able to turn it into body speed. I couldn't believe how fast my legs were moving, and I'm sure the fans had the same sentiment.

I could tell that Basso was thinking that also from the fear that he showed on his face. As he continued to run, I continued to chase, then when he slowed down for just an instant to catch his breath, I threw a left hook to his ribs and followed up with a right cross to his jaw that completely demolished him.

His tall muscular physique collapsed like you were looking at one of the twin towers when it fell.

The referee didn't even bother to count. He immediately waved his arms that the fight was over. The way that Basso hit the canvas, everyone was concerned that he might be seriously injured.

When the referee waved his arms that the fight was over, I turned to my corner, with one baseball eye and the other with a two-inch gash, that gave me a bloody face, I yelled out, DESTINY!

By the time I yelled out that word, Dom, Tom, and Luz were already upon me, right behind them was John, Mark, and Richie. Looking back, it felt like one of those Rocky movies.

When the announcer ran into the ring and stuck a microphone into my bloody face, he asked the question, what do you have to say after this being your toughest fight? I responded, "I did have a concern about this fight after I realized that I didn't have enough spinach in my pre-fight dinner.

Before the announcer could ask another question, Dom grabbed me by the shoulders and said to the announcer, "That's it, we're taking him to the hospital to get stitched up."

Richie being my PR man, immediately took over the interview, and started to answer the questions from the announcer, as all the guys started to escort me to the dressing room.

At the same time, Basso was being escorted out of the ring also, but he was leaving on a stretcher. It turned out that we were both taken to the same hospital around the corner from the Garden.

After they checked my vital signs and gave me ten stitches above my left eye, the hospital released me. Basso was not so lucky; he spent the next three days in that hospital. They found him to have three cracked ribs and a broken jaw.

As we were leaving the hospital, Tommy surprised me when he said, "We're going a few blocks away, to the Fairmount Hotel. There are 200 families and friends in their ballroom waiting to celebrate with you."

Driving over to the Fairmount, I asked Tommy the question, "What if I lost, and was seriously hurt?" When Tommy stumbled for words on the question, Luzzi bailed him out when he said, "Destiny, my good fella, destiny." Tommy then said, "That's right, destiny is my answer."

When we arrived at the hotel and then began to enter this large lavish and elegant room, everyone started to applaud me.

I then walked over to this small platform. Standing upon it was a podium with a microphone.

Reaching for the microphone I said, "For anyone who might care, I'm ok. I received ten stitches above my left eye, my right eye is swollen to the size of a baseball, and I incurred bruising all around my face."

"The good news is the doctor says I will be fine with plenty of rest and lots of sex."

There is one more question that I would like to answer for you, without you having to ask. "I had no energy left, if I didn't get him when I did, I would have lost."

The only answer that I have to all of these crazy things that have been happening is DESTINY!

When I walked off the platform, my kids were the first to hug me. I must say, my biggest surprise was when my publisher, Don McGuire, came over to hug me. He told me that he caught a flight from Phoenix, Arizona to New York City and arrived just in time for the fight.

Although we have only met once face to face before tonight. That was when I promised Don that I would go out to see him with a bottle of Johnny Walker Blue and a box of Cuban cigars.

This man is a very special and important person in the fulfilling of my destiny. He is the man that has been chosen to bring forth the message from Beyond the Beyond through his publishing company.

As I began to get tired, Tommy hit me with another surprise. Along with the booking of the ball room for the night, Tommy also booked our entire entourage to stay here at the Fairmount for the next two days.

I was truly elated to hear that news. I had a really bad headache from being peppered from that hard-stiff jab hitting my head, along with that, my entire face was starting to hurt.

Knowing what Tommy said, I decided to go to my room at once to lie down. I was disappointed because I really wanted to talk to Marie. I haven't spoken to her since I've been home from prison.

I was very happy to see that Tom invited her and her friends.

My two brothers were going to escort me to my room, until my brother, John, opened the door to the ballroom and discovered a large gang of reporters waiting on the other side of the door.

My brother, John, immediately closed the door behind him and then we went to gather our entire entourage.

Luzzi was dancing with his wife, Maryann, Dom was talking to my publisher, Don and Richie was talking to Marie's girlfriend, Donna Brocco, Tommy was already with us.

Once all the guys were together, we left the ballroom. Seconds later we were stormed by reporters that were trying to get to me.

The entourage had me surrounded as we walked fast toward the elevator to get to my room.

During that time, Dom kept screaming, "We're staying here tonight, I promise all of you we'll do an interview tomorrow morning. Come back tomorrow morning, we will be here, wait for us in the lobby tomorrow morning."

Once we made it to my room, I told all the guys, "Go back down to the party and have a good time, I'll be alright." As all the guys were leaving, my brother, John, insisted that he was staying, what could I do, you can't tell your older brother what to do.

It really didn't matter; in a short time, I was snoring and out like a light. It was then that my brother decided to leave and join the party.

Once John entered the ballroom, he went directly to the platform, grabbed the microphone from the podium and said, "The Doc is fine, he's sound asleep, snoring like a baby."

The party went late into the night, or should I say, it went early into the morning. The next morning the guys told me that everyone had a great time.

Before my kids left, they went up to their Uncle John for reassurance that I was ok. John told them that he would have me call them tomorrow.

Being that we all had our own separate rooms, mine being the exception with a suite. Tommy and Luz were able to have their wives stay over; the girls were looking to do some New York shopping the next day.

The next morning, we were all going to have a meeting in my suite at 9:00 a.m. The meeting was delayed for a while being that both Tom and Luz showed up late. Perhaps they were getting a little before they sent their wives out shopping.

When Tommy showed up, he came in laughing. He then said, "My wife left to go shopping. When she hit the lobby, she realized that she forgot her reading glasses so she came back up to the room for them. That's when she told me that the lobby is full of reporters."

Hearing that, I said, Dom gave his word last night to the reporters for an interview, so I asked Richie, would you please go down to the lobby and tell the press that we're having a meeting, as soon as the meeting has been completed, we will come down for the interview.

As Rich was leaving, I called him back, and then asked my brother, Mark, to bring the message to the reporters. I told

Rich to sit back down, and then after taking a sip of coffee, I began to speak.

I started by saying, "Guys, I've been very lucky with all my fights till last night. Last night I got beat up, I hurt all over; I was cut for the first time in all of my fights. Nevertheless, I was so very blessed to have won the fight."

"Thank God my next and final fight will not be for at least three to four months from now. That will be enough time for my cut to heal. You guys and destiny have brought us here with one final step away from winning the heavyweight championship of the world."

Turning to Dom, "I said, I want you to write this down, I humbly say, but I know that we're in the driver's seat, and don't allow anyone to tell you different."

"I have three demands, and they must be met, this is non-negotiable. The fight must be held at Met-Life which is Giant Stadium in the Jersey Meadowlands. I must be guaranteed one hundred million dollars for this fight. My last demand is that the fight must take place within the next four months."

"If any of those demands are not met, I'm retired. Fellas I have already achieved my goals. I have the name recognition that I need to begin my last final quest in life."

"I will not go into this fight and risk my life to fight an opponent that is impossible to beat. He holds the greatest record ever at 55 and 0, with fifty-two knockouts. Jamel Perry is six foot eight inches, weighs 280 pounds and is solid muscle. He has a reach that has never been seen before in the history of boxing. This is why my demands must be met."

"I tell all of you in truth, the champ has no choice but to meet my demands. There is no one out there that could earn him more money in one fight than I can. Not only will I get

$100 million, I'm sure he's going to get even more. He knows there is no way that he could get that kind of money without me. Most important the promoters know this; they also know that they are going to break the record of the Mayweather-McGregor pay-per-view fight for the largest grossing fight ever."

I then told the guys, "If the fight is made, and I know it will be, this is what I want. I guess you could say that this is my final will and testament in case I don't survive the fight."

I then turned to Tommy and said, "Please write this down. I want each of our entourage, you, Luzzi, Dom, Rich, John, and Mark to be given a check for two million each. I want Louise, Angie, and Marie to receive a check for two million. I want my four children, Paul, Gina, Marcus, and Brian to receive a check for one million each. I want each of my eleven grandchildren, Else, Isabella, Ava, Alexandria, Olivia, Gina, Sophia, Charlie, Marcus, Luke, and Baron to receive a check for one million. I then instructed Tommy to allocate two million for Dom to put together a new boxing gym naming it in the honor of both him and my father. He will be the sole owner of the facility. Last by not least, I need you to write a check for five million to Kim, who has been so loyal to have stayed with me all these years helping me fulfill my destiny."

"To wrap up this meeting, what I'm telling all of you, there is much to celebrate because, win or lose, what I asked of Tommy will be done."

At that moment Rich said, "Doc, I have a question for you. I can understand your demand for the money you're asking for. Knowing and understanding your mission in life, I can see why you put a time frame on the fight. What I don't understand is why you put a demand on the fight being held at Met-Life Giant Stadium?"

My answer to Rich was, "I have had a vision for the longest time that I would be speaking in front of 100,000 people at Giant Stadium, perhaps this will be the opportunity to fulfill my vision."

"We're now all going to go down to the lobby to keep Dom's word by doing the interview. Once we entered the lobby, all the reporters rushed to me, that's when my brother, John, in a stern voice said, "Don't crowd him, he'll answer all your questions, one at a time."

The first question asked of me was, "Did you feel that there was any surprise in your fight with Basso Bear?"

I said, "He fought the exact fight I anticipated. In fact, that's the reason why after the press conference, the day before the fight, I decided to go to Katz's famous deli. After hearing Basso's game plan, I needed some cheering up. Katz's corn beef and pastrami did the job."

The next reporter's question was, "You looked extremely frustrated out there, you were being beaten up, you couldn't get to him."

"I could not have said it any better, I had very little left, and my only chance was to put all my energy out of me at once in hopes that I could get to him.

Once I heard the next reporter start to ask a question about Jamel Perry, the undefeated heavyweight champ, I stopped him and said, "Hopefully I'll answer your most important questions about fighting the champ."

"The champ needs me; I don't need the champ. The promoters need me, I don't need them. I could retire today. I have a far greater and important challenge still ahead of me in my life other than chasing the heavyweight championship of the world."

"The promoters need me more than any other opponent for the champ. Fight fans around the world want to see this fight more than any other fight."

I then said to the reporters, "Write these demands down, these are my demands to make the new dream fight of the century, and the largest grossing fight ever."

"I must be guaranteed 100 million dollars, the fight must take place in four months, and the fight must take place in Met-Life Giant Stadium."

"These are my demands to fight the greatest heavyweight champion ever. To walk into the ring against him, I will truly be risking my life."

"I'm sure you now want to hear my opinion of the fight. I truly believe with all the logic that I can muster, that I don't even have the slightest of chances to beat this invincible hulk of a man."

"Yet I know there will be many dreamers out there. There will be many rooting for the underdog. There will be many wanting to see the impossible. There will be many hoping for the miracle."

How could anyone be so naïve? It's because of who we are as human beings that gives us the ability to have hope, gives us the ability to believe and the gift to dream.

After my last statement, I decided to leave the rest of the questions to Rich. I told the reporters that any further questions could be answered by my PR man, Rich LaManna.

The rest of the guys escorted me back to the suite, as Rich stood there solo and answered all the remaining questions.

When we returned to the suite, Tommy told us that there was a message telling him that our entire entourage would be going tonight to the play that's about Frankie Valli and the Four Seasons.

All the guys were overjoyed hearing that news. They grew up in our neighborhood and their music was our music.

That play has been the hottest ticket in town for some time. I guess it just shows what being a celebrity can do.

After Rich completed the interview and returned to the suite, we all decided, being that it was a nice day, to take a walk on Broadway to Time Square.

I must admit, although I felt guilty, trying to stay humble, it did feel good to be recognized and acknowledged by so many.

Most showed concern over the injuries that I displayed all over my face. I guess if they realized the money that I received, they would gladly trade my injuries for the check I received.

I guess the crowds that I drew convinced me that I accomplished my objective. Later that night we all enjoyed the play and the music. It offered so much nostalgia to all of us and the songs brought back so many memories.

I'm sure all of us would agree that this turned out to be a perfect weekend.

The next morning before we checked out of the hotel, to head back to Jersey, we all had breakfast and then a meeting.

It was agreed that I was going to take only one week off and just rest before I would slowly go back into training.

My first instructions were to Rich when I told him to orient my brother, John on the process of elimination that you did so far on purchasing me a two-bedroom condo.

I then turned to John and said, "Make a choice within the next week, pay cash, and then get the entire condo furnished."

Now turning to Tom, Luz, and Dom, I let them know that they were in charge of negotiating and making the deal for the fight. I made them aware that they had to have this deal completed within the next two weeks.

I informed Richie that he was needed to assist these guys in making this deal. Turning to my brother, Mark, I let him know that his job for the next week was hanging out with me.

When I returned to my son's house, I called my kids to reassure them that I'm ok. I must say, I couldn't have been greeted any better than the surprise my daughter-in-law, Amy, prepared for me.

She cooked my special creation, chicken pepperoni. I taught her how to make it. Although I hate to admit it, she makes it better than I do.

It took me much longer than I wanted it to be, but on the third day back. I went to my house of worship to give thanks.

That special place is The Sacred Heart Church of Lyndhurst, New Jersey. This is the house where my mother went to pray. This is the place that I went as a little boy to find my creator. This is the place that I went as a man to ask for the forgiveness of my sins.

I now come to this place to ask for the strength to keep myself humble. I now ask for the strength not to be changed from fame and wealth. I now come to this place to ask for the strength to stay focused so that I can fulfill my purpose.

The next few days worked out exactly like I planned. My brother Mark and I did nothing but chill. We went out for breakfast, lunch, and dinner, we tried to get my brother John to come, but he was too busy taking care of getting me a condo and getting it furnished.

Mark and I went to my grandkid's basketball games, went to see my son coach his high school basketball team, and found time to see my niece, Maria, Mark's daughter, perform in a high school concert.

The next day we took off and went to spend the day shooting the dice and watching the little white ball spin round and round on the roulette table at the Mount Airy Resort and Casino. My friends, Jimmy Tuthil and Dennis Arcelleta run the joint.

The next day while my brother, Mark, nephew, John and I were having lunch, my brother got a call on his cell phone, it was Tommy. He asked where I was, Mark told Tommy, "He's here with me at the Lyndhurst Diner." Tommy said, "Keep him there, I'll be there shortly."

Mark then said to me, "That was Tommy, he sounded really excited, he said for us to wait for him, don't leave."

Approximately forty-five minutes later, there are four very emotional guys headed toward our table. It was Tommy, Luzzi, Richie, and Dom.

They all started to talk at once, that's when I stopped them and said, "Take the empty table next to us and slide it over to the side of our table."

I then asked Tommy, "What's going on?" He replied, "We did it, they made the deal, they met all our demands."

Richie then jumped in and said, "They were being tough, not wanting to budge off their last offer of 95 million, until Luzzi said, not meeting Doc's demands works out for me, I have him tied up with a movie and book deal, why should he risk his life getting in the ring with that killing machine."

Tommy then said, "After hearing what Luzzi told the promoters, they collapsed like a ton of bricks, as they said, "Ok you have what you asked for."

Dom then said, "The fight is scheduled to be held three months from this upcoming Saturday at Giant Stadium."

After Dom made that statement, I didn't comment. Not commenting puzzled the guys. That's when Tommy said, "Doc, you don't seem happy."

My response was, "I thought it would take two weeks to make the deal, you guys closed the deal in a week." When I started to laugh, all the guys started to laugh.

That's when Luzzi made the comment, "Oh my, I might become the co-manager, co-trainer to the heavyweight champion of the world!"

That brought laughter from all of us, even though the thought of that could become a reality.

Dom began to take charge again when he said, "Ok fellas, tomorrow we all go back to work." Dom expressed to me the concern that he had, knowing I would be unable to spar for the first two months of my training; I had to allow the healing process to take its course. Dom was also aware that I still had some swelling on my right eye.

Rich then interjected that we would be having a press conference on Thursday morning, which is only two days away. It will be for the contract signing and announcement that Doc will be fighting Jamel Perry for his championship crown.

After Rich gave the announcement, I informed the guys that I will be going into seclusion immediately after the press conference until fight time. I informed Rich that he will be in charge of all the public relations just like last fight.

When the next day arrived, the limo was there with our entourage to pick me up. Today I start my training for my last fight, win or lose.

After starting back on my training yesterday, the next morning came quick and I had to be up and about early since today was the press conference to announce the contract signing for the fight.

It was being held in New York City at the luxurious Plaza Hotel overlooking Central Park.

Not just our country, but the entire sports world has an interest in this upcoming event.

When the limo pulled up to the front of the Plaza, and I exited the vehicle, I was surrounded by reporters. They followed me into the Plaza ballroom where the press conference was being held.

When I entered the ornate room, the champ was already sitting with his entourage on the dais. Just from the first glance at him, I could tell that he wasn't very happy that I was receiving all the attention.

After they had me seated side by side with the champ, as we both were signing the contract for the fight, I looked like I could easily be his grandfather.

When the reporters asked a few questions to the champ, he had very little to say. I would think that if you had the best record in the history of the heavyweight division at 55-0 with 52 knockouts, there is no need to say much.

I had even less to say than the champ. I sure didn't want to say anything that might upset this gargantuan of a man.

Truth be told, neither one of us had to promote this fight, the public wanted to see this fight more than any other fight in the history of boxing and the promoters knew it.

I'm sure you could say that this was substantiated when the first hour that tickets went on sale the fight was sold out. With seating being put on the entire football field, the crowd will top a little over 100 and 3,000 fight fans.

Nevertheless, because the champ and I didn't really have much to say about the fight, the champ's trainer started to talk shit to Dom about the fight.

I believe that Dom read right through him, that he was doing this not to disappoint the TV and newspapers even though the fight was already sold out.

So, Dom played along. They started off by disagreeing on who hit harder, the old man or the champ. Dom and the champ's trainer then started to argue if I would even be able to hit the champ being that he's so tall and has an incredible reach over me.

That's when Luzzi jumped into the conversation by saying to the champ's trainer, "Oh yeah, look what Doc did to

Basso Bear, the former champ, and he was even faster than your fighter."

Apparently, that statement by Luzzi really irritated the champ because he got up and walked to the other side of the dais, he then put his fist right up to Luzzi's nose, as he said, "How would you like for me to knock you out?"

Luzzi's response was, "No, no, no, you got it all mixed up champ," as he started to point to me, he then said, "He's the fighter, not me, go knock him out, I just became a grandfather."

Not only did Luzzi's statement bring much laughter from both camps it also had the news media hysterical with laughter.

On the way back from training later that day while riding in the limo, the TV was showing the news conference from that morning. When they started to show Luzzi's scene, everyone started to laugh all over again.

This time I said, "Thanks Luz, put the heat on me."

Luzzi's response was, "Did you see the size of that guy, he's bigger than the hulk. I signed up to be the co-manager with Tommy, not the fighter."

We all started to laugh all over again from Luzzi's remarks.

As the weeks went by the cut above my eye was healing even faster than we anticipated. During those few weeks that had passed, my brother, John, was able to purchase a two-bedroom condo for me.

He had paid cash for it, had it completely furnished, and had me immediately moved in.

The timing was perfect for me to have moved into that condo. Although my son and daughter-in-law made me feel so comfortable, and it was great being around my grandkids, it was time for me to have the privacy to prepare for my journey.

One day coming back from training, Luzzi mentioned that our close friend, Robert, called him wanting to know if we could make it for lunch on Thursday.

I told Luzzi to call him back and tell him yes.

When Thursday arrived, Robert showed up late for lunch. That gave Luz and me a chance to talk. I told John that even though I feel so thankful, because win or lose, I have already succeeded in rewarding all my close friends, and family with the benefits of my achievements.

I let Luz know that I still feel pressure because my competitive nature wants me to win this championship, not just for myself, but for everyone around me.

It was then that I confided in John when I said, "Luz, I never feared anyone, and I always felt I could beat anyone in a fight, regardless of how big or strong they may be. I know that's from the positivity and confidence that I have always had in myself throughout my life. John, I'm only telling you now for the first time, my logic and common sense tell me that I don't have a chance, not even one in a million."

Before Luz had a chance to answer me, Robert walked into Steve and Andrea's Luncheonette. After we all hugged, the first thing I said to him was, "You're my Mayor, I just moved into a condo I bought in Lyndhurst."

For the next two hours, we did nothing but laugh. Those old stories never get too old to have us stop laughing and enjoying them. I would say that this is a special gift that all friends share.

Now that I had the tranquility of being alone in my condo, I was able to get back to my writing.

I guess it would be hard for anyone to believe that I'm looking forward to getting back to public speaking even more than fighting for the heavyweight championship of the world.

After another month had passed, I have been doing nothing but training hard, doing my meditating and writing, along and staying in seclusion. I decided to tell Dom that I'm taking a day off.

Without telling anyone, I jumped into my car and drove to the Mount Airy Resort and Casino. After having lunch with a few of the bosses, I went to spend the rest of the day playing the games of chance.

As I began to drive back home, I was on Route 80 in Mt. Pocono, Pennsylvania when another incredible event took place.

I saw a car hanging off a cliff with just the tail end of the car hanging on by a rock.

As I started to pull over, there were a number of other cars that had already pulled over. Those people were trying to help to no avail.

The car was a two door, there were two bodies in the vehicle, both in the front. Just the angle that the car was hanging off the cliff, it was impossible to get to them.

The dilemma was the rock that was stopping the car from falling off the cliff was starting to loosen. When I noticed that the rock was just about to break, my emotions became so stirred up, that I grabbed the back bumper as I began to scream the word, "DESTINY."

With an incredible burst of energy that felt like thunder from the sky, I literally lifted the car back up off the cliff with my bare hands.

When the people there started to attend to the driver and the passenger, his young son, I took off. Just like the two other incredible events that took place, as I took off you could hear the siren coming from afar to the scene.

Not to my surprise, when I turned on the eleven o'clock news that evening, the incident that occurred earlier that evening was all over the news.

Eyewitnesses were telling how out of nowhere, this old man came running onto the scene, he then literally with his bare hands lifted back up a car that was hanging off a cliff to save two lives.

The incident took place on Route 80, in Mt. Pocono, Pennsylvania.

The news reporter was trying to tie this incident with the two other stories of an old man, with superman strength, that came to the rescue by turning an overturned truck back onto its wheels on Route 46 in Little Falls, New Jersey, and the other story where an old man came onto the scene of a burning car on Federal Highway, in Boynton Beach, Florida and with his bare hands ripped off both doors on the car to save two lives.

I'm sure that everyone I know is hearing all about this event that took place in Pennsylvania. I sure am happy that I never told anyone where I went today.

The next day after that escapade yesterday, I went to the big house to see the boss and give thanks for literally being given the strength to be able to rescue that father and son.

I know that there is so much I need to pay back, and I'm eager to begin as soon as I can get past this last fight.

We are still one month away from this big event and I am starting to become anxious. I'm also starting to notice that the anticipation of the fight is beginning to distract me from my writing.

That was an immediate message to me to stop my writing for now. I will resume only when the time comes that I'm inspired to do so.

So, I decided that I'm going to eat, drink, and sleep with this fight on my mind. I'm going to prepare myself to do whatever it may take to win this fight and become the heavyweight champ.

I want to do this for my father's memory. Growing up, he was always my inspiration and I already know that his spirit will be with me.

I decided that I will not allow any negative thoughts to enter my mind. I will not allow myself to think that the impossible cannot be done.

I've decided that I will do whatever it takes to win this fight including risking my life. I am ready to die if this is the choice of my destiny.

My mind had gone into such a deep thought, that when I came out of it I was on the scale the day of the fight at the weigh-in.

After the weigh-in and our physical, being that it was only 12:30 in the afternoon, and being that my condo was only ten minutes from the stadium, I decided to go back home to hang out.

The champ who is from South Carolina has been staying at the Plaza Hotel in New York City the last two months. He has been doing his running in Central Park. The Plaza had set up a boxing gym for the champ right in the hotel.

Rather than going back to the Plaza, the champ decided to hang out in the lounge of the locker room.

Main event fighters, especially for big fights, usually come to the arena four hours before their fight, which is about two hours before the fight card begins.

For no particular reason, I decided to come to the stadium when the fight card had already begun.

When the limo pulled up to the stadium, thousands of fans were still entering the stadium. The limo then pulled up to the VIP entrance, and our entourage exited the limo.

When the fans noticed that I was in the group, they started to yell my name.

Once we entered the Stadium, we were escorted to the Giant's locker room. The champ had already spent a good part of the day in the visitor's locker room.

Even though I wasn't the champ, being I knew the people who run the Stadium, they made sure I was given the home locker room. The only advantage between the two locker rooms was the luxurious coach's lounge that was part of the home locker room. That was the place our entire entourage stayed waiting for the fight.

After first looking at his watch, Dom then gave the signal, and Tommy and Luz came over to tape my hands. As they were doing their job, I said, "This is the last time you guys will be taping my hands."

I told them, "You guys have really become experts on taping hands." Luzzi responded, "That's why we're the best manager-trainers around, we're going to win the heavyweight championship tonight."

I looked into both their eyes as I said, "I know that you're not lying."

Once the guys completed taping my hands, I went over to Dom and said, "I'm going to lie down on one of the couches and meditate, please don't have anyone interrupt me. Come get me when it's time.

As I was resting with my eyes closed, my first thought was, I'm about to walk out into this Stadium that is seating well over 100,000 people that have come to see me do battle.

I would have preferred they had come to hear me speak, but nevertheless, the feeling is awesome.

MY NEXT THOUGHT WAS TO MY CREATOR, THE SOURCE OF ALL MATTER AND ENERGY IN THE UNIVERSE, AND ALSO THE SOURCE OF MY DESTINY.

I then prayed that if it was destined for anyone to be seriously hurt in this battle between two warriors, let it be me and not the young man.

My mind then began to question if this super-strength would enter my body. Not only do I know that it will be impossible to win this battle without it, I'm also feeling that even with it, the task at hand may be too great.

Wanting to test my emotions, I began to think of the greatest words ever said to me. It was when I received a letter from my ex-wife, the mother of my four children.

In the letter she expressed her sentiment with these words, "Of all the men in the world, there is no other man that I would want to be the father of my children than you."

Before I had completed those words in my mind, the tears just started to flow; it was hard to control my emotions so no one in the coach's lounge would notice.

My final thought before I heard the words from Dom, "It's time," was from my teaching on positivity. So, I got up from the couch, went to my luggage, and dug for my book, "The Great Escape."

After tearing through the pages, I found what I was looking for on page 160. I then began to read what I had written in the middle of that page.

"I have lived my entire life with positiveness. I tell you in truth that to always maintain positiveness throughout your life is the secret that will guarantee you to achieve the most of what you're capable of achieving."

I now give you the greatest secret to success in life and that is positiveness and optimism. No sooner than I told myself, *"I can beat him,"* Dom walked over to me and said, "It's time."

After hearing that, I asked my brother, John, for my glasses, I wanted to clearly see the pageantry like my last fight at the Garden.

Just before taking my first step to enter the Stadium, I turned to my brother, John, and said, "You're son, Joey, is up there with daddy, I'm going to whip this young man for them, just pray that I don't hurt him."

After saying those words, we both started crying. Would you believe that when I started to take the long walk to the ring, I was bawling like a baby, as Frank Sinatra was singing, "My Way," on the sound system.

As I continued to walk toward the ring, the sound level was deafening. I was truly in awe as I looked out to see the massive amount of humanity.

As I was getting closer to the ring, I started to see more and more celebrities. I guess Tommy was right when he said there will be more celebrities here tonight than for any other event ever.

By the time that I climbed the steps to enter the ring, Frank Sinatra had just completed singing, "My Way," on the sound system.

Once in the ring, I discovered something that I never experienced in my other eight fights. I was completely relaxed, I wanted to fight, despite who I was about to fight.

As the champ was entering the ring, I was busy looking out into the crowd for Jennifer Aniston. When I did look at the champ, he was impressive looking, his size and reach were incredible, but surprisingly, it no longer affected me.

Strangely, I wasn't having a concern if I would be receiving this super-strength entering my body.

When the referee called the two combatants to the center of the ring, and I had to stand face to face with the champ, you had to question how the judges would even allow this contest to continue.

I guess you would have to say when the public has a demand for something and it involves tremendous amounts of money, one way or another, it's going to happen.

After we received our instructions and I walked back to my corner for my mouthpiece and to wait for the bell to ring for round one, I felt sorry for Dom, Tommy, and Luzzi. They had looks on their faces of guilt like they were sending me out there to be slaughtered.

I then turned to Luzzi and whispered in his ear, "Tell Tommy and Dom not to worry, I'm going to beat this young man, my concern is not to seriously hurt the champ."

When the bell rang, as I went toward the champ ready to block his stiff left jab, I was surprised with a straight right hand that dropped me to one knee.

After that, you just knew what everyone in the Stadium was thinking, *why did they even allow this fight to take place.* Most felt they were about to see the lion eat the gladiator in the Colosseum.

I got up after the count of eight and said to myself, *"Shit, he hits hard,"* as I immediately started to throw left hooks and right crosses just to keep him away from me.

Those punches did not hit their target being that he was so tall with that incredible reach, but nevertheless, the champ had to respect my punching power.

From the start of the second round, after I threw a right cross and dropped the champ to one knee when he got up, he started to dance and stick that long stiff jab into my face the rest of that round.

As I was sitting on the stool waiting for the third round to start, I said to myself, *"The super-strength has not entered my body.* I know that to be true because the way I hit the champ if that super-strength was within me, the champ would have never gotten up for at least a while.

When round three started and the champ began throwing that stiff jab into my face, I knew I was helpless. I knew that if I allowed that to continue, I was going to get completely chopped up.

I then came up with a strategy, every time he started to throw a left jab heading to my face, I countered with a left hook, not trying to hit his jaw, but hitting his left arm as it was extended from throwing the jab.

From the start of the fourth round, I was able to see that my strategy worked, because he stopped throwing that incredible left jab. If I was unable to accomplish that, I knew that I wouldn't have remotely had a chance.

The remaining time of the fourth and the entire time of the fifth, I pressured the champ trying to knock him out. I paid the price dearly by having my face battered and all cut up.

At the end of the fifth round, when I returned to the corner, not only did I know that I had very little left, but the guys could also tell. That's when they all simultaneously said, "Do you want us to stop the fight?"

Hearing that question, I asked the guys, "What round is coming up?" Tommy replied, "It's the sixth round." My response was, "Thank God, my mother's birthday, the sixth. I'm going to win the championship on the round of her birthday."

When the bell rang for the sixth round, the guys saw a young man go out to battle, despite what his face looked like.

I started to throw left-right combinations nonstop. It didn't matter where my punches were landing, as long as they were above the belt. My barrage of punches continued to hit him everywhere, his arms, shoulders, his waist, solar plexus, head and jaw, I was even punching his fist.

Halfway through the round, he finally collapsed into submission and I became the heavyweight champion of the world, at Giant Stadium, in front of more than 100,000 screaming fans.

As I was thanking the fans, before getting ready to speak to them, as I'm saying, thank you, thank you, God bless you all, thank you so much, I heard my daughter, Gina, screaming at the top of her lungs, "He came to, he's alive."

Immediately I saw my entire family and close friends enter this large room. There were my four kids and their spouses, all my grandkids, my two brothers, my niece and two nephews, and my close friends, Luzzi, Tommy, and Robert.

Even the three loves of my life were there, Louise, Angie, and Marie.

As everyone surrounded me as I lie there in the bed, I asked the question, "So I didn't win the heavyweight championship. What… did the champ knock me out?"

That's when my son, Brian, said, "Dad, what are you talking about? You have been in a coma and on life support for the last year and four months." My son Paul then said, "Dad, your four kids made the decision, after conferring with the doctors, that today we were going to pull the plug. Today was going to be your wake."

I then turned to my friends, Tommy and Luzzi and said, "Where is Richie?" When they looked confused over the question, I said, "LaManna, Richie LaManna." That's when Tommy said, "Richie LaManna, I haven't seen him in almost sixty years since high school."

I turned to Luzzi and said, "Luz, you and Tommy weren't with me on my boxing journey to the championship over the last year?" Luz responded, "Doc, you have been in a coma for the last year and four months."

I then asked my brother, Mark, "was it true that I was jumped by three inmates and I beat them all and sent them to the hospital with broken bones?" His answer was, "That's all true, but you left out the fourth inmate, he was the one who hit you from behind with a heavy-duty steel pot. That gave you a concussion and put you into a coma and life support."

One last question Mark, "Is it true that there were two bent bars in the area of the fight?" Mark's response was, "Yes, they're still investigating that, they are calling that a real mystery."

I then turned to Marie and asked, "Is it true that I won my 440.10 motion and was released from the overwhelming evidence that my lawyer provided?"

Marie answered in a very somber tone when she said, "No Doc, your motion was denied, you have been in a State prison nursing home all this time."

I have one last final question for all of you. You say that I've been here in a coma and on life support for the last year and four months. You say that I haven't been moved during this time

"Is it true that one year ago, on Route 46 in Little Falls, New Jersey, that a truck was turned onto its side, and the driver was about to die, and witnesses said an old man came out of nowhere and turned the truck right side up with his bare hands and saved the truck driver's life?"

Is it true that six months ago on Federal Highway in Boynton Beach, Florida that two people were saved while being trapped in a burning car when this old man came out of nowhere, and with his bare hands ripped both doors off the car to save the young couples lives?"

Is it true that only one month ago on Route 80 in Mt. Pocono, Pennsylvania, there was a car hanging off a cliff with a father and son in the car? There was a rock that was logged at the tail end of the car that was keeping it from falling off the cliff. As the rock began to loosen, this old man came onto the scene and with his bare hands lifted the car back off the cliff.

In all three cases, eyewitnesses claim that it was an old man, perhaps a superman, but in all cases, he was never found.

Everyone in the room was aware of all three of those phenomenal stories. Those stories were on the news all over the country, in hopes to find the mysterious superman.

My son, Marcus, then said, "How could my father have known about all those stories if he's been in a coma on life support during all this time?" His mother, Louise, then said,

..."This perhaps, might be one of the great mysteries of all time."

About the Author

ccording to the FBI and New York Organized Crime Task Force, Paul "Doc" Gaccione is a leading member of the Mafia.

In 2010, he was arrested and charged for a murder that occurred twenty years earlier. He was released on a million-dollar bail for two years until he was convicted in 2012. He is presently serving a twenty year to life sentence. He claims his innocence and is presently in the appeal process.

He is the author of *"Beyond the Beyond:"* My Journey to Destiny, which hit the Amazon bestseller list, and *"The Godfather of Souls,"* Barnes and Noble's five star rating. Also acclaimed for *The Great Escape:"* The Inside Story of the Dannemora Prison Escape and *"The Psycho Club."* Continued reader demand has spawned *"The Fighter."*

Paul "Doc" Gaccione was born and grew up in Lyndhurst, New Jersey. An amateur boxing champion and weightlifting champion who excelled in athletics, he became a leader in the physical fitness industry. He holds a Doctorate in Naturopathic medicine and is the inventor of a body building stop watch.

He has also spent many years as a motivational speaker. He's the proud father of four children and eleven grandchildren, and his principal beliefs are "To demand respect, you have to give respect" and "No man should ever raise his hands to a woman."